Will Samantha and Tor live

The phone rang, and Tor went into the kitchen to answer it. He was gone for several minutes, and when he returned to the living room, he had a dazed look on his face.

"What is it?" Samantha asked, jumping up from the sofa.

Tor's expression was serious, but his eyes were bright. "You're not going to believe this," he said. "That was Jimmy Hollis, Sammy."

"Is everything all right?" she asked. "Are Hannah and Ghyllian okay? Did something happen to Finn?"

Tor shook his head. "Things are going really well for them. They've decided to close the bed-and-breakfast."

"Oh, no!" Samantha exclaimed. "Where will we stay when we go back to Ireland?"

"They're in the process of expanding the farm," Tor went on, "building new barns, and Jimmy is going to spend more time on breeding flat-track racehorses. He wants to raise a colt that will run in the Kentucky Derby someday."

"That's wonderful, but where will we stay?" Samantha asked again.

"That's why he called," Tor replied. "He asked if you and I would be interested in moving to Ireland to run the eventing part of the farm. How does that sound to you?"

Collect all the books in the Thoroughbred series

Collect all the books in the Ashleigh series

*coming soon

THOROUGHBRED

SAMANTHA'S IRISH LUCK

CREATED BY

JOANNA CAMPBELL

WRITTEN BY

MARY NEWHALL

HarperEntertainment
An Imprint of HarperCollinsPublishers

F
Cam

📖 **HarperEntertainment**
An Imprint of HarperCollins*Publishers*
10 East 53rd Street, New York, NY 10022-5299

Produced by 17th Street Productions,
an Alloy Online, Inc., company.

HarperCollins books are available at special quantity discounts for bulk
purchases for sales promotions, premiums, or fund-raising.
For information please call or write:
Special Markets Department, HarperCollins Publishers Inc.,
10 East 53rd Street, New York, NY 10022-5299.
Telephone: (212) 207-7528. Fax: (212) 207-7222.

ISBN 0-06-059525-6

HarperCollins®, 📖®, and HarperEntertainment™
are trademarks of HarperCollins Publishers Inc.

Cover art © 2004 by 17th Street Productions,
an Alloy Online, Inc., company.

First printing: August 2004

Printed in the United States of America

Visit HarperEntertainment on the World Wide Web at
www.harpercollins.com

❖ 10 9 8 7 6 5 4 3 2 1

1300392

*For Frank and Nancy's beautiful
granddaughter, Talia*

SAMANTHA'S IRISH LUCK

"DO YOU THINK THIS ROOM IS GOING TO BE BIG ENOUGH?" Samantha Nelson asked her husband, Tor. They were standing in the middle of the spare bedroom in their house at Whisperwood, the Kentucky eventing farm they owned. It was early October, and outside the window a large oak tree spread its branches, afire with leaves of russet, gold, and auburn. Fat brown acorns dangled from their stems, ready to fall to the ground. Beyond the tree, Samantha could see Whisperwood's grassy paddocks, where Thoroughbreds and warmblood horses grazed. Miss Battleship, their big chestnut broodmare, stood at the gate to her turnout, watching Kaitlin Boyce, one of Whisperwood's riding students, lead Sterling Dream to an adjoining pasture.

Kaitlin paused to pet Miss Battleship, and Sterling crowded close to the fence, hanging her gray head over the top rail to greet the other mare before Kaitlin led her to her own paddock. Samantha smiled and glanced at her husband, who was by her side, gazing out the window.

"I like the view from this room," Tor said. "Can you imagine a better way for our children to wake up every morning than to see the horses? It's going to be a great nursery, Sammy."

For the past six years the bedroom had been used for storage, and Samantha and Tor had crammed unused furniture, boxes full of memorabilia, and old clothes into the space until they could find the time to sort things out. Giving riding lessons, breeding and training sport horses, and competing in three-day events and steeplechases gave them little time to spend fixing up the ranch house. Taking care of their horses and maintaining the riding facilities and stable had been their priority, until they learned they would be having a baby early in the spring.

It had been a wonderful surprise for the Nelsons the previous week when Samantha's adoptive sister,

2

Cindy McLean, and their friends Ashleigh Griffen and Christina Reese had taken a day from their own busy schedules to help clear the room in preparation for the baby.

"I like the view, too, but we need space for all the furniture," Samantha said. "The room looks huge without anything in it, but I'm still not sure it's going to be big enough." She rested her hands on her rounded stomach. Her voice seemed to echo off the walls of the empty bedroom, but Samantha knew that once the nursery was finished, it would feel cozy and welcoming. She was looking forward to seeing the room full of baby furniture. "Do you think we need to fix up one of the bigger rooms instead?" she asked Tor.

Tor looked around the empty space and shook his head. "Babies are small," he said. "They don't need a lot of room."

"Maybe at first." Samantha pushed a lock of her wavy auburn hair behind her ear, then cocked her head to gaze up at her tall, blond husband. "Babies may be small," she said, "but they need lots of things that take up room."

"We'll make it work," Tor told her. He pointed at one wall. "The changing table can go over there," he said.

Samantha pointed at the wall where the bare window let in the soft autumn sunlight. "Rocking chair over there," she said, then sighed. "It's going to be a little cramped."

"Hey, Sammy, we're ba-a-aack!"

At the sound of Christina Reese's voice, Samantha went to the door and stuck her head in the hallway. "We're in the nursery," she called.

In a moment Christina, Ashleigh, and Cindy came down the hall, and Samantha stepped back to let them into the room.

All three women were dressed in jeans and T-shirts, looking ready to start working. Cindy and Ashleigh both sported baseball caps advertising Whitebrook, the farm where Ashleigh and her husband, Mike Reese, bred and trained Thoroughbred racehorses, while Christina, Ashleigh's eighteen-year-old daughter, had a bandanna tied over her long reddish-brown hair.

"Promoting your competition?" Tor asked Cindy with a teasing grin, pointing at the Whitebrook cap.

Cindy set down the bag she was carrying and reached up to touch the hat. "We haven't had any cool hats or shirts printed up for Tall Oaks," she said. "Besides that, Whitebrook is *friendly* competition. But

I do think it's time I talked to Ben about having our own hats and jackets." Cindy, a retired jockey, managed Tall Oaks for Ben al-Rihani. Ben had owned the Thoroughbred breeding and training facility for only a year. With Cindy's expert help, he was busy building up the breeding stock and reestablishing Tall Oaks as a successful farm after saving it from bankruptcy.

Christina set down a large cardboard box full of plastic drop cloths, sticks for mixing paint, masking tape, paint rollers, and brushes. She nodded toward a bag sitting on the floor near the closet. "There's the paint we brought last week when we cleaned the room out," she said. "We can spread these cloths over the floor and start painting." She propped her hands on her hips and looked around the room. "I know exactly what colors go where," she said. "I'm ready to go to work."

"She's been poring over home-decorating magazines all week," Ashleigh told Tor and Samantha. "This baby is going to have the most colorful nursery in Kentucky."

"What do you want me to do?" Samantha asked, reaching for a package of drop cloths.

"Nothing," Cindy said, snatching the plastic

sheets from her sister's hand. "You're going to leave the house while we paint."

"We'll get started as soon as you go," Ashleigh said. "We don't want that baby exposed to paint fumes, and you don't need to do anything." She looked around the room. "There's barely room for the three of us to work in here as it is."

"What about me?" Tor asked. "I'm tall. I can reach the ceiling."

"It's under control," Ashleigh said, wrinkling her nose at him. "We all may be short little jockeys, but if you'll bring in a ladder for us to use, we'll manage just fine." Like Cindy, Ashleigh had retired as a jockey, and now she worked with Samantha's father, Ian McLean, Whitebrook's head trainer. Together, Ashleigh and Ian trained Thoroughbreds for flat-track racing and were extremely successful.

"Speak for yourself," Christina said to her mother, pulling herself up to her full height. "I'm almost five foot six. I'm a *tall* jockey." Christina raced regularly, fitting her time on the track between the college classes she was taking. She and her own three-year-old Thoroughbred, Wonder's Star, had won the Belmont Stakes the previous spring, and now she was training another colt, Royal Blue, in the hopes of making the bay yearling Whitebrook's next Triple Crown champion.

"I know you're tall," her mother said. "That's why you're going to paint the ceiling." Ashleigh turned back to Tor and Samantha. "We do need a screwdriver to take the switch plates off the walls, so if you'll get us one to go with the ladder, we can get started on this room."

Tor hooked his arm around Samantha's shoulder and urged her toward the door. "It sounds like you have things under control," he said good-naturedly, grinning at Ashleigh. "I'll leave Sammy at the barn and bring back some tools for you."

"I'm going, I'm going," Samantha said, letting Tor move her out of the room. "I can take a hint, you know." She looked back and smiled at her three friends. "Thanks for all your help."

"No problem," Cindy said, peeling the wrapping off a paint roller. "I'm looking forward to visiting my first niece or nephew in this nice colorful room we're fixing up."

Samantha started to respond, then clamped her mouth shut. "I'm getting out of your way now," she said, and followed Tor down the hall.

"When are you going to tell them?" Tor asked as

he opened the front door of the house for Samantha.

"About the big news?" Samantha asked him. She stopped on the covered porch of their single-story house and gazed out across the yard toward the large covered arena. "When they're done fixing the room the way they want," she said. "It'll be a nice surprise."

Tor nodded. "I'm going to grab a screwdriver and the ladder for the three fairy godmothers, then I need to set up the arena for this afternoon's riding classes. And no," he added as Samantha started to open her mouth, "you can't help me, either. You need to find a comfy place to settle down for a while and rest." He patted her stomach. "You need to take good care of yourself and that precious cargo you're carrying."

Samantha twisted her mouth, then exhaled. "Fine," she said. "I won't feel guilty about being lazy. I'm going to go visit with the horses."

"Just don't pick up anything heavier than a carrot," Tor said in a warning voice as he headed for the shop, where he kept his tools.

Samantha crossed the yard to the long stable attached to one side of the indoor arena. Since most of the horses had been put out for the day, the barn was quiet. The wide aisle had been swept clean, and when she glanced in the stalls she saw that each one was filled with fresh bedding. The water buckets had been scrubbed and filled, and the hay nets and feed pans were neatly stacked in a wheelbarrow in preparation for feeding later in the day.

Kaitlin's been hard at work, she noted with a smile. A high school senior, Kaitlin had started helping at the stable in repayment for riding lessons on Sterling.

Buying the gray Thoroughbred jumper from Christina and been one of the best moves Samantha had made. Before Christina had decided to focus on racing, she and Sterling had been top-class eventing competitors. Because of Christina's work with Sterling, the mare was well schooled in arena jumping, dressage, and cross-country, the three aspects of three-day eventing. Now Kaitlin was developing her own skills with the experienced mare and proving to be a solid eventing competitor herself.

Samantha saw Kaitlin at the far end of the barn, standing in front of Finn McCoul's stall. She walked past the empty stalls to where the seventeen-year-old was feeding the huge stallion a slice of apple.

"The barn looks wonderful," Samantha told Kaitlin. "You're doing a great job."

"I like doing this kind of work," Kaitlin said, petting Finn's long brown nose. The stallion bobbed his head, lipping at Kaitlin's hand in search of another treat.

"He's a bit greedy, isn't he?" Samantha said fondly, petting Finn's sleek, muscular neck.

"He's awesome," Kaitlin said, gazing at the massive horse's deep, broad chest. "He's the tallest horse I've ever been around, except for some draft horses."

"I fell in love with this guy the first time I saw him," Samantha told Kaitlin. "I couldn't believe it when Tor brought him over from Ireland."

"How old was he when you first met him?" Kaitlin asked.

"Haven't I bored you with that story?" Samantha shook her head. "I thought everyone knew how we got Finn."

"I knew you spent a long time in Ireland, but I never heard why you came back or how you ended up with Finn," Kaitlin replied. "Do you have time to tell me about it?"

Samantha nodded. "I've been kicked out of the house for a while, and Tor won't let me as much as pick up a flake of hay." She sighed.

"Well," Kaitlin said, eyeing Samantha, "if those are the rules, you'd better stick to them. I don't want to have to tell Tor you were cleaning stalls or anything else."

Samantha shook her head. "With everyone keeping such a tight rein on me, I don't have a choice," she said. "Which means I have all the time in the world to tell you about Finn."

"Great," Kaitlin said. She ducked into the barn office and grabbed a folding chair, which she opened in front of Finn's stall. "You sit there." She shifted a large wooden tack box so that it was facing Samantha, then plopped down on it, her hands clasped together, an eager look on her face. "Now tell me about Finn," she demanded. "I want to hear the whole story."

"Okay," Samantha said, leaning back in the chair. Finn hung his head over the stall door, snuffling at her hair, and Samantha lifted her hand to stroke his nose affectionately. "He's such a good boy," she said fondly. "Anyway, just before our wedding, Tor and I spent all the money we'd saved for our honeymoon on Miss Battleship, so we didn't think we'd get to go on a trip."

"Good," Kaitlin said. "She's given you some really great foals."

Samantha nodded. The big chestnut mare, a descendant of Man o' War, had never been successful as a racehorse, but the foals she had dropped, all sired by Finn, were consistent winners on the steeplechase and cross-country courses. "She and Finn have done well by us. We never regretted buying her."

"But you got your trip anyway," Kaitlin noted.

"We sure did," Samantha said. "The big wedding gift our friends and family gave us was a month in Ireland on an equestrian vacation."

"Wow," Kaitlin said, her eyes wide. "A whole month of riding in Ireland. It must have been the most perfect honeymoon ever."

Samantha nodded. "It was wonderful."

"But you stayed there for six years?" Kaitlin asked.

"I'm getting to that," Samantha said, smiling.

"Okay, I'll quit interrupting so you can tell me the story." Kaitlin stared intently at Samantha.

Samantha opened her mouth to speak, but gasped as her belly gave a sudden lurch. "Feel this," she said, taking Kaitlin's hand and pressing it to her side.

Kaitlin's eyes widened as she felt the movement under her hand. "What was that?" she asked.

"A knee or an elbow, I would guess," Samantha said, settling back as the activity inside her subsided. "It's getting a bit crowded in there, I'm sure." She sighed and leaned back in the chair. "And I still have months to go. I sure have a lot more sympathy for the broodmares now." She gazed at Kaitlin and smiled. "But we were talking about twelve years ago, weren't we?"

"Yes," Kaitlin said. "You were saying you went on your honeymoon in Ireland. Then you didn't come back for six years?"

"That isn't quite how it worked out," Samantha said. "We came home after our honeymoon, but it was on that trip that I first met Finn."

2

TWENTY-THREE-YEAR-OLD SAMANTHA LOOKED OUT THE jet's window, awestruck by the sight of Ireland's rugged coastline. "I can't believe we're really here for our honeymoon," she said breathlessly, unable to tear her gaze from the dramatic view of the tall cliffs battered by the rough, gray Atlantic Ocean, the heathery green bluffs rising high above the water, and the wide swaths of beach stretching for miles along the coast.

"Do you want me to pinch you?" Tor asked, leaning across his seat to share Samantha's view as the plane started its descent over the island.

"I don't think so," Samantha replied. "If I'm

dreaming, I don't want to wake up." The plane banked, and Samantha could see the interior of the island, stretching green far into the distance, with rivers snaking like silver ribbons along the ground and the clusters of whitewashed houses looking like toy villages in the distance. "Wow," she murmured, then turned to look at her husband. "I guess I should move my head so you can get a better look," she added, leaning back.

Tor patted her knee. "Watching you so happy is worth everything I'm not seeing," he said.

Samantha laughed, shaking her head. "I am a little giddy about it," she admitted, taking another look out the window. "But can you believe this? We're in Ireland, Tor."

"For four weeks," he affirmed. "A month of horseback riding on the beaches."

"A month of exploring the Irish countryside," Samantha added.

"A month of enjoying Irish culture," Tor continued.

"A whole month at an equestrian bed-and-breakfast," Samantha concluded. "We have the most wonderful family in the world to do this for us."

Tor nodded. "The best," he agreed.

The flight attendant's voice came over the intercom. With her lilting Irish accent, she instructed the passengers to buckle up and prepare for landing, and soon they were coming down on the runway of the Shannon airport. Samantha and Tor filed off the plane, joining the throngs of travelers at the luggage pickup, and before long they were reunited with their baggage.

Samantha looked around the busy concourse. "Now what?" she asked, stepping out of the way as several harried-looking people passed them. She watched travelers being greeted by friends and family, and businesspeople with raincoats flung over their arms rushing toward the escalators that led to the parking garage. "I wonder where we're supposed to meet our ride to Celtic Meadows."

Tor pointed toward a nearby escalator, where a short, stocky man wearing a canvas barn jacket and a tweed cap was holding up a sign and looking around at the milling crowd of people. "I think I see our chauffeur over there."

As Samantha looked at the man, he turned in their direction, and she could read the words *Nelson* and *Celtic Meadows* printed in bold black letters on the sheet of paper he was holding. She and Tor picked up their suitcases and walked over to him.

"I think you're waiting for us," Tor said.

"You'd be Mr. and Mrs. Nelson, I take it?" the man asked, his soft brogue making the words sound almost musical to Samantha.

"That's right," Tor replied with a smile, setting his luggage down. "I'm Tor Nelson, and this is my wife, Samantha."

"I'm Jimmy Hollis," the man said, stuffing the paper in his pocket and reaching out to shake Tor's hand. "Owner of Celtic Meadows, where you'll be staying. *Cead mile failte.*"

"'Kade mela foylta'?" Samantha repeated, giving him a quizzical look.

Mr. Hollis gazed at Samantha, and his face split into a wide grin. "A hundred thousand welcomes," he translated. "You look a bit Irish yourself, young lady," he added.

"My maiden name is McLean," she said, extending her hand.

"That's a fine name for sure," Jimmy Hollis said, the word *fine* sounding like "foyn." "I know some good, honorable folks named McLean. You're no doubt related in some way."

He reached for Samantha's baggage. "So you'll be staying with us for a good bit, will you now?" He tipped his head toward the escalator. "I'm sure you'll be wanting to get settled after your trip, so we won't dawdle here any longer. This way to the car." He turned, and Samantha and Tor fell into step behind him.

Mr. Hollis glanced over his shoulder when they reached the rows of parked cars. "We'll be driving about an hour to the farm," he said. "My lovely wife will have a nice bit of food waiting for you there, and you can take a rest, or you can stroll through my barns and fields if you like. It's a good way to wind down from the long flight."

After they had stowed their luggage in the trunk, Samantha and Tor settled into the backseat, at Mr. Hollis's insistence. "You're on your honeymoon," he said to Tor. "The last person you want to be sitting next to is an old curmudgeon like me when you have your darling Irish lass to hold hands with."

Samantha shot Tor an amused look, and they sank back on the soft seat of the car to enjoy the passing scenery. Once they had left the busy area around the airport, they drove through the Irish countryside, passing cottages and large, stone-fenced fields. Samantha saw several small, compact horses grazing in the pastures, and she craned her neck to check out the stocky animals.

18

"Connemaras," Jimmy Hollis said, pointing out the sturdy build of Ireland's indigenous breed. "The most versatile breed imaginable. No one truly knows their origins, but they're as much a part of Ireland's history as the ancient Celts themselves."

In other pastures, small sheep grazed, and Samantha gazed at the meadows full of the woolly animals, in colors ranging from creamy white to gray, brown, and black.

"Those are our Shetland breed," Jimmy said in explanation. "Much like the Connemaras, they're hardy little creatures, bred to withstand our harsh environment, with wool as fine as frog's hair and soft as butter." He glanced toward the backseat and caught Samantha's eye. "You'll be wanting your darlin' husband to take you shopping for one of the local spinsters' hand-knit sweaters," he said. "You'll be glad of it when it gets damp."

"Damp in the summer?" Tor asked.

"Ireland gets rain up to two hundred and seventy days a year," Jimmy told them. "That's what helps keep it all so nice and green."

Some distance from the road, Samantha could see a tall stone pillar in a field filled with more sheep. The spire pointed toward the sky like a lonely finger.

"What is that?" she asked, staring at the ancient monolith.

"That would be a menhir," Jimmy Hollis said. "A long stone, you'd call it. They were monuments, some folks figure, to mark special occasions or events, or possibly to mark distances. It's all lost in history, what they were actually used for." As they continued along the road he pointed out a group of massive stones set in a circle. "The stone rings have even a bit more mystery to them," he said. "It's been guessed that they were used to predict the seasons or for clan gatherings, but other people claim they were meant for pagan rituals, and it isn't a bit odd to see fair folk dancing among them when the moon is full. There are plenty about."

"Fairies?" Samantha asked, staring at the strange ring of stones.

Jimmy shot a grin over his shoulder. "The circles, I meant," he said. "But then again, when it comes to Ireland's mythical folk, like leprechauns and fairies, you never know. When you're out riding the land, you'll come across strange things, some of them quite unexplainable." He paused, then sighed. "But then, who needs a dull scientific explanation for everything? Sometimes a bit of legend and imagination can make something mundane quite mystical."

He turned onto an unpaved road, slowing as a shepherd urged his flock of sheep across the road. They passed several more pastures of grazing horses, and Samantha looked closely, admiring the solid build of the horses.

"Plenty of our finest hunters have Connemara blood in them," Jimmy said. "You can see it in their conformation. There's no better foundation for an eventing horse than to have Connemara pony in its lineage."

Mr. Hollis fell silent for a few minutes, and though Samantha tried to stay alert, not wanting to miss a minute of the new things she was seeing, her eyes grew heavy. The next thing she knew, Tor was nudging her arm. "We're at the farm," he said. "Time to wake up, sleepyhead."

Samantha rubbed her eyes and stretched her neck, then climbed slowly from the car and stared at the large, whitewashed stone house they had parked in front of. "This is the quaint Irish cottage?" she asked, looking up at the twin turrets, roofed in red tile, that faced the circular drive.

"It keeps the rain off our heads." Mr. Hollis pointed at one of the turrets. "That's to be your accommodations," he said, pulling Samantha's suitcases from the trunk. "You're our only visitors this week, and we were plainly told you'd want a view of the horses and pastures from your window, so that's the way it is."

Samantha turned to look around the land surrounding the Hollis home, drinking in the view of the rolling, white-fenced pastures, the low, weather-worn hills in the distance, and the big-boned horses grazing near the long stone stable. Gray clouds filled the overcast sky, hanging low over the farm and outlying land, but even with the threat of rain in the air, the area had a magical, ancient quality.

"This is the most perfect place I've ever seen," she said, suddenly filled with the strange sense that this was exactly where she was meant to be.

"Ireland's been called a wee bit of heaven by many," Jimmy Hollis said. "Now come in and meet my wife, Hannah, and enjoy a spot of tea."

Samantha and Tor followed Jimmy into the house, walking directly into the large kitchen. A plump, dark-haired woman was standing at the oven, checking the contents of a large pot, and the scent of freshly baked bread filled the air. Lively fiddle music was coming from a radio on the counter, and Mrs. Hollis was singing along with the raucous lyrics, bobbing her head in time to the music.

As they came into the kitchen she broke off her song in the middle of a word, a bright smile on her round face. She set her spoon down and wiped her hands on her apron, then hurried across the kitchen's flagstone floor to greet them.

"Come in and sit for a spell," she said, gesturing for Samantha and Tor to leave their luggage in the doorway. "Jimmy can tote your bags to your room while you have a mug of nice strong tea and a fresh scone."

Before they could protest, Mrs. Hollis was urging them toward a big wooden table, and Jimmy left the room with their suitcases.

"As soon as you've had a bit of refreshment," he said over his shoulder, "I'll take you out to meet the horses."

"Thank you," Samantha murmured as Mrs. Hollis poured tea from a ceramic pot into mugs and set them in front of Samantha and Tor.

"Call me Hannah," their hostess said. "And if you call Jimmy anything other than just that, he'll ignore you." She pushed a plate piled with fragrant, raisin-studded scones toward Tor. "Eat up," she said, sinking onto one of the empty chairs and helping herself to a scone. Following her lead, Tor and Samantha spread the sweet triangles with butter from a crystal dish and with jam that Hannah explained she had made herself, "after me girl, Ghyllian, picked the berries."

"Delicious," Samantha said, taking a second scone. The tea was dark and strong, and Samantha added a generous amount of cream and sugar to it, while Tor drank his black.

"Now then," Jimmy said when he returned to the kitchen several minutes later, "are you fortified enough to visit the barns, or are you thinking of taking a little rest first?"

"The barns," Samantha and Tor said in unison.

"Then the barns it shall be," Jimmy said, gesturing for them to follow him.

As they crossed the yard to the large stable, Samantha looked at several of the big-framed horses in the closest field. "Irish Thoroughbreds," she said, admiring a deep-chested black standing close to his paddock fence.

"The finest horses in the world," Jimmy said proudly. "Our main business here at Celtic Meadows is breeding and training racehorses and jumpers. Hannah enjoys visitors and she loves to cook for people, so it made sense to open our home up as a bed-and-breakfast as well. My own passion is for the flat track, but we keep a few steeplechasers as well. Ghyllian takes our guests on cross-country tours on horseback. Most prefer the slow and steady saddle horses, but we do have a few decent jumpers if your skill level allows."

"What an ideal setting," Tor commented, gazing at the craggy hills in the distance. He took Samantha's hand as they followed Mr. Hollis out to the large barn.

Jimmy pointed at a hedge of spiny brush along the drive and glanced over his shoulder, offering them both a toothy smile. "As the old saying goes," he said, "when the gorse is in bloom, it's time to be kissing. Of course," he added, "since it blooms spring and fall, there aren't many times of the year that aren't right for giving your darling a little peck on the cheek."

Tor and Samantha laughed, and Tor leaned over to press a light kiss on Samantha's cheek. "Like that?" he said.

Mr. Hollis nodded approvingly. "Just so." He pointed at a spacious, white-fenced paddock, where half a dozen horses were relaxing. "Those would be my visitors' horses," he said. "Each of them well trained and gentle as a lamb. You can look them over and choose which horses you'll want for your mounts while you're here."

Samantha gazed at the large warmbloods, taking in the conformation of each of them as she leaned against the paddock fence. She pointed at a well-muscled, flea-bitten gray gelding. "He looks like he knows how to take a fence," she said.

Mr. Hollis looked at the horse, then glanced back at her with raised eyebrows. "You do know your horses, then," he stated. "Colm there is one of the best cross-country jumpers in the bunch. We only let experienced riders use him."

Tor stood quietly, eyeing the various horses, then pointed out a long-legged black with a thick mane that fell on both sides of his neck. "That fellow looks fearless," he said. "And like he might have some speed."

"Again, good call," Mr. Hollis said, a grin stretching across his ruddy face. "Night Sky, we call him, and in his younger days he ran in the steeplechases at Punchestown racetrack in Kildare. He was a fair steeplechaser in his time." The farm owner turned and narrowed his eyes as he looked at Samantha and Tor. "What is it you haven't told me about yourselves?" he asked, folding his arms in front of him.

"Well," Tor said, "we were both raised on Kentucky horse farms. Horses are our lives." He explained that they both worked at Whisperwood.

"Ah," Mr. Hollis said, understanding clearing his

expression. "So you'll let me see how you handle my mild-mannered fellows, and then we'll see if you're fit for something a little more spirited." He gestured for them to follow him, and strode past the paddock and around the barn.

As Samantha rounded the corner, she stopped abruptly. In a nearby paddock stood a heavy bay mare. The mare had the solid conformation of a jumper, well over sixteen hands high, with flat knees and large feet. In spite of her size, she was graceful-looking, with an air of gentleness that made Samantha want to slip into the field and rub her long, mahogany-colored nose.

But even more attention-grabbing to Samantha was the dark brown foal at her side. The colt snapped his head in their direction. He pricked his dainty ears in their direction, his eyes wide and alert, his nostrils flared as he took in their scent. Samantha stared at the sturdy weanling, unable to tear her gaze away.

"Who is that?" she said, her voice a breathless whisper.

"That would be Kerry Maid," Mr. Hollis said. "She's one of my finest broodmares, blessed with an outstanding disposition, and always drops a stout, healthy foal."

As Samantha watched, the colt took two steps in their direction, leaving his dam behind as he examined the visitors. His eyes locked with Samantha's, and she felt a shiver run through her, as though the colt was communicating directly to her.

"Her young one there is a son of Red Rum," Jimmy added.

"The same Red Rum who won the Grand National Steeplechase three times and placed second twice?" Tor asked, looking from Mr. Hollis to the foal.

"That would be him," Mr. Hollis said proudly. "The little scamp is as bold as can be, just like his sire." The colt took several more steps toward them, his eyes bright with curiosity.

"He's been very gently handled," Mr. Hollis explained. "I want my horses to be trusting of humans, so my girl and I spend time with them every day, from the minute they're born, making sure they get the best of treatment."

Samantha watched, entranced, as the colt looked back at his mother, several yards behind him, then looked to the fence, where the three humans were watching him. He tossed his head, then broke into a springy trot, his short, curly tail flagged as he came the rest of the way to the fence.

Samantha hung her hand over the top rail, and the colt came straight to her and stopped, then pressed his warm, soft nose into her hand, letting her cup his muzzle in her palm.

"We don't feed them by hand," Mr. Hollis said. "Not at this young age. I've found they can get a bit nippy, and I don't want to have to undo any bad habits."

"That's a good idea," Tor said. "How do you reward them?"

"My Ghyllie lavishes so much attention on them that if it were food, they'd all be big as elephants," Jimmy said with a chuckle.

Once he had taken in her scent, the little brown horse stretched his neck up, resting his chin on the rail, and Samantha began scratching his furry baby coat, running her fingers lightly along his silky neck.

"What's his name?" Samantha asked, her eyes still locked with the colt's.

"Ah," Mr. Hollis said. "His name is Finn McCoul. He's the best weanling on the place, and one I have great hopes for."

3

THAT EVENING WHEN THEY SAT DOWN TO DINE WITH THE Hollises, Samantha felt so at ease, it was almost as though she were in her own family's kitchen back in Kentucky. She sat back and listened to Jimmy and Tor discuss training methods for steeplechase horses. After the long flight, she felt too tired to join in the discussion, and her mind was stuck on Finn McCoul. With one look, the colt had captured her heart.

"In my younger years I was a decent flat-track jockey," Jimmy told them. "I miss it sometimes, but as long as I can keep training racehorses, I'll grow old happily."

"Where's Ghyllian?" Hannah asked as she carried a large soup tureen to the table.

"She'll be along shortly," Jimmy said, nodding at a fifth place setting. "She took one of the three-year-olds out for a bit of cross-country riding, but you know she isn't going to miss one of your fine suppers."

Hannah glanced at Tor and Samantha and shook her head. "She's as fanatical about the horses as her father," she said fondly. "I've told them both I should just move my oven into the barn, or we should move the horses into the house."

As she sat down at the table, the kitchen door banged open, and a girl of about fifteen raced into the house, her long dark hair tousled and her eyes bright. "I'm back!" Ghyllian Hollis announced, peeling off her barn jacket while she shoved the door closed behind her with a booted foot.

"We'd never have known if you hadn't told us," Hannah said, then pointed at the empty plate on the table. "We're waiting supper on you, missy."

Ghyllian caught her lower lip in her teeth. "Sorry," she said. "Pennywhistle and I had such a grand ride." She looked at her father and grinned. "I took her on a new trail," she said. "She went just like you said she would, not hesitating at a single fence, Dad. You have to let me race her at Kildare."

"We'll discuss that later," Jimmy said. "Right now

31

you need to wash up quick-like and take a seat. When you're not going full tilt we'll introduce you to our guests."

Ghyllian shot a broad smile at Samantha and Tor, then darted out of the kitchen. Hannah exhaled softly. "She's a bundle of energy, that girl of yours is, James."

"That she is," Jimmy agreed, pushing the soup tureen in Samantha's direction. "Dish up, Samantha. Ghyllie will be back in a flash."

Samantha could hear the affection and pride in Jimmy's and Hannah's voices, and she smiled. "You must think the world of her," she said, ladling beef and barley soup into the bowl in front of her.

"Without any doubt," Hannah replied.

In a minute Ghyllian was back at the table, her hair brushed and her face and hands scrubbed clean. "Welcome to Celtic Meadows," she said to Samantha as she sat down. "I hope you like horses."

"Oh, just a little," Tor said with a grin.

"The Nelsons breed horses in the United States," Jimmy said. "You don't have to worry about being burdened with a couple of beginners here, Ghyllie." He looked from his daughter to Samantha and Tor. "When we have raw beginners as guests, Ghyllian has to slow down and stick to the easy trails."

"Boring!" Ghyllian exclaimed, filling her own bowl with soup. "I'd rather take the advanced riders cross-country." She took a bite and grinned at her mother. "You outdid yourself, Mum," she said. "I don't think I've ever tasted better."

"I'd pass my recipe on to you," Hannah said. "But you'd feed the barley and carrots to the horses and wonder why the soup tasted off."

Ghyllian shrugged and looked at Samantha, her eyes twinkling. "She's right," she admitted. "I'd just as soon spend my days in the barn cleaning stalls as cook a meal."

"Me too," Samantha said, instantly liking Ghyllian, with her bright eyes and quick smile. "What's your favorite type of riding?"

"I love cross-country," Ghyllian said without hesitating. "More than anything, although I do like working with the flat-track horses, too."

"That's great," Tor said, taking a slice of freshly baked bread from the basket in the middle of the table. "Maybe you can show us some of your favorite cross-country trails."

"Absolutely," Ghyllian said, digging into her bowl of soup enthusiastically. "There are miles of fences and fields we can ride, and then there are the beaches to gallop on, too."

"We're going to have a great time here," Samantha said.

Tor looked at her and nodded. "I think," he said, "you are absolutely right."

After filling up on a traditional Irish farm breakfast the next morning, their plates heaped with sausages that Hannah called bangers, sweet bread she told them was barm brack, bacon, and eggs, Tor and Samantha left the farmhouse and headed for the stables. A light rain was falling, and Samantha pulled the hood of the yellow slicker that Hannah had given her over her head.

"Jimmy wasn't kidding about the rain," Samantha commented. "I hope we get at least a few days of sun while we're here."

"We will," Tor said confidently, stuffing his hands into the pockets of his own raincoat.

When they got out to the barn, Ghyllian had saddled the gray gelding that Samantha had admired and the black that Tor had singled out, along with four other horses, including a big bay mare.

The girl looked a little grim as she tightened the girth on a smaller bay gelding. "We're not riding alone today," she said, sounding disappointed. "A group of tourists from Holland is coming in for a day of riding. That means I have to babysit." She patted the bay gelding's nose. "But that doesn't mean you two can't go riding off. I'll give you a map of some of my favorite spots if you'd like."

"That's very sweet," Samantha said, then glanced at Tor with a slight frown.

Tor picked up another saddle and set it on a chestnut gelding's sleek back, then shook his head. "I think we'd rather have you show us your favorite sites," he told Ghyllian. "Today we can take the easy trails along with you and the other guests." He tightened the girth. "We've got plenty of time to ride while we're here."

"Are you sure you don't mind?" Ghyllian asked, her eyes lighting up. "I would so love to go just with you two."

"We'll wait for tomorrow," Samantha promised, picking up a bridle.

"Then today we'll ride down on the flats," Ghyllian said. "It isn't too dull, but we can't take off galloping or do any jumping."

"It might be just as well for us to take a leisurely ride today," Tor said. "The truth is, I'm a bit thrown off by the time change and the long trip yesterday."

"Me too," Samantha said quickly.

When the three tourists arrived in their rental car, Samantha smiled to herself. The middle-aged man and two women were wearing brand-new jodhpurs, tall boots, and heavy jackets, and all three had strong Dutch accents.

Ghyllian greeted them warmly and introduced Samantha and Tor as "American equestrians here for a visit." The other guests—Anna, Sophie, and Rolph—had very little riding experience, so Ghyllian quickly ran through the riding rules for the newcomers and paired each of them up with one of the rental horses.

When Samantha saw that their guide had every-thing under control, she mounted Colm, then rode the gray over to where one of the women, Sophie, was balanced uncertainly on Mickey, the small bay.

"Press your heels down," Samantha suggested. "It'll sit you deeper into the saddle."

"There's nothing deep about this saddle," Sophie said nervously, but she did what Samantha had told her, and offered a cautious smile. "I think that helps," she said.

"You'll be fine," Samantha said. "I'll ride beside you."

"Thank you," Sophie replied, tangling her fingers into the gelding's thick black mane.

"Relax a bit," Samantha said. "You'll get the feel for it quickly."

As they rode away from Celtic Meadows, Samantha saw that Tor had befriended Rolph, who seemed a little more comfortable on his horse than the two women. Ghyllian was in the lead on the bay mare, with Anna at her side, and they ambled down the lane at a leisurely pace.

Ghyllian pointed out an ancient Irish tomb called a dolmen, two large rocks with a flat rock resting on top of them. Samantha gazed at the stone marker, standing in the middle of a rock-bordered field.

"Lots of Ireland's historical monuments are on private land," Ghyllian explained. "There are sites like that scattered throughout the country." As they rode on she talked at length, describing the local plants and wildlife and sharing a bit of Irish lore, bringing the history of the area to life. Samantha could tell that Sophie was unwinding a little as Mickey plodded calmly along the dirt road.

"You have a natural seat," Samantha said encouragingly. "The only way to improve it is to spend more time on horseback."

Sophie flashed her a smile. "You make it look so easy," she said. "I know my muscles are going to be as sore as can be when we get back to our hotel in Dublin."

Samantha nodded in understanding. "I'm sure they will," she said. "I ride almost every day, sometimes for hours, but if I get away from it, I still feel it in my muscles."

Ghyllian led them through a break in the hedge that lined the road and onto a trail that led toward the low, grassy hills to the east.

"What is that rocky hump over there?" Tor asked, pointing toward a large dome rising from the ground.

"That would be a cairn," Ghyllian said, riding toward the monument. "They were used for a number of things, and some have stones inside that are covered with ancient drawings symbolizing the four seasons. This one is quite plain. There's a story that it was built centuries ago for an Irishwoman whose only love sailed across the seas in search of gold, never to return. They say she is still here, waiting for him to come home."

Samantha felt a shiver run down her spine, and

she looked around slowly, almost expecting to see the ghostly image of the woman wandering around the ruin.

A sudden gust of wind whipped over them, and a eerie keening sound filled the air, seeming to come from the cairn itself.

Sophie jumped. "What was that?" she exclaimed, involuntarily jerking the reins and clapping her legs to Mickey's sides. Mickey tossed his head in response, and Sophie cried out as the bay bolted away from the cairn, his rider clinging helplessly to his mane.

Without a second thought, Samantha brought Colm around and urged him into a gallop, chasing after the runaway horse. Samantha leaned forward, eyeing the ground in front of her for the safest route. The bay was galloping straight toward a crumbling rock wall in the distance. Samantha knew that Sophie would never stay astride the horse if he tried to jump the fence.

Colm's strides were long, and Samantha felt the damp wind in her face as they raced across the rocky ground. The big Irish Thoroughbred didn't seem to have any problem with the rough footing, so Samantha asked him for more speed. Colm lengthened his strides, galloping surely, leaping small mounds and quickly closing the gap between Mickey and him. Samantha veered him to the left, hoping to get ahead of Mickey and Sophie so that they could cut the bay off before he unseated his rider.

Soon they were even with the other horse, and Samantha crouched over Colm's pumping shoulders, asking for even more speed. When they dropped down into a hollow, Samantha saw a huge stone at the bottom of the decline, and she tried to move Colm around the obstacle. The trained jumper held his course, running straight at the boulder.

He's going to jump it! Samantha thought, sucking in a deep breath. If anything happened to the horse, she would never forgive herself. But it was too late to change direction now, so she shifted her weight into jumping position, bracing herself against Colm's muscular neck. She held her breath as they sailed over the rock, heaving a sigh of relief when the gelding cleared it and bounded up the hill. To her dismay the stone fence was only a few strides away, but when she glanced to her side, she saw they were well ahead of Mickey and Sophie. But now that Colm had seen the rock fence, he tried to head for it, determined to make the jump.

"Oh, no, you don't!" Samantha cried, pulling his

head firmly away from the wall. She angled him so that they could get in front of the runaway, and as Mickey neared them Samantha used Colm to force the other horse to turn, moving him away from the dangerously close rock fence.

She reached out and caught Mickey's flapping reins, slowing the bay down to a bouncy trot, then to a walk. To Samantha's relief, Mickey stopped calmly. He looked around, released a loud breath, then touched noses with Colm. White-faced and shaken, Sophie gripped the gelding's mane with trembling fingers.

Samantha hopped from her horse's back and quickly ran her hands along Mickey's legs, but other than having broken into a sweat from his run, he seemed fine.

"We could have been killed!" Sophie exclaimed. "Why did he do that?"

Samantha shrugged. "You gave him all the right cues," she said, then explained about the aids Sophie had used to tell Mickey to gallop. "But," she said, grinning at the other woman, "you're a much better rider than you realize. You stayed in the saddle. You did great, really."

The woman swallowed hard, then nodded. "I guess I did pretty well, didn't I?"

"Do you want me to pony you back, or do you feel like handling him yourself?" Samantha asked, still holding Mickey's reins. "I'll stay right beside you in case he gets frisky."

"Then I'll ride back on my own," the woman said, collecting the reins. They walked back at a leisurely pace, and by the time they reached the rest of the group, Sophie seemed calm and much more confident about being able to stay astride her horse.

"That was some excellent riding," Rolph said, looking from Samantha to Sophie.

"Wasn't she amazing?" Samantha asked, nodding toward the woman, who sat a little taller in the saddle.

Ghyllian worked her jaw, looking anxiously from Samantha to the three tourists. Samantha winked at the girl and shook her head. "Everything is fine," she mouthed to their guide.

"All's well that ends well," Sophie said, patting Mickey's sweaty neck. "I'll have a fabulous story to tell when we get home, won't I?"

They rode back to the farm, where Ghyllian escorted the visitors to their car before she began untacking the horses.

"That was awful," she said to Samantha when she

returned to the barn, where Samantha and Tor were grooming Colm and Night Sky. "None of the horses has ever done anything like that before."

"It was the timing of the ghost story," Tor said, smiling at Ghyllian. "When you finished telling about the lonely Irishwoman, and then the wind made that whistling noise on the stones of the cairn, Sophie clamped her legs into Mickey's sides and tightened the reins, so he did what he was told." He ran his hand down the little bay's shoulder and nodded approvingly. "He sure knows how to move, I'll say that for him."

"I won't ever tell that story again," Ghyllian said, pulling the saddle off Mickey's back. She looked at Samantha. "Thank you," she said. "That was some wild ride you took, too."

"If I hadn't been so worried about that poor woman, it would have been a lot of fun," Samantha said, patting Colm's neck. "He's really an awesome horse."

Ghyllian nodded. "You sure brought out the best in him."

As Tor pulled the saddle from one of the other horses, Ghyllian raised her hand in protest. "You're supposed to be enjoying yourself here," she said quickly. "I'll take care of the horses, and you two go for a stroll or have some tea and sandwiches. My mum will have some food set up for you at the house."

"We'll help you out here first," Tor said. "We never ride without taking care of our animals."

Samantha nodded firmly. "I like grooming the horses," she said. "Don't chase us away now."

After they had put the horses up, Samantha and Tor enjoyed another of Hannah's meals. Then Samantha wandered out to the paddocks while Tor went out to the stable to see some of the other horses and meet the farm's three employees. Finn McCoul was with his dam, Kerry Maid, but when Samantha approached the fence, the colt immediately came up to her.

"Someday you'll see him racing in the Grand National," Jimmy said from behind her.

Samantha turned and smiled at the colt's owner. "I believe it," she said, petting Finn's soft brown nose.

"Go on in with him," Jimmy urged her, unlatching the paddock gate.

Samantha stepped into the paddock, and Finn stayed close to her, letting her run her hands down his sturdy legs, feeling the slope of his shoulder and the curve of his neck. His baby hair was soft under her hand, and the colt lipped gently at her as she petted him. When Finn gazed at her with his soft, dark eyes, she felt again that strange sense that he was communicating with her. She looked into his liquid eyes, murmuring softly as she stroked his soft coat.

"He seems to connect well with you," Jimmy commented. "Feel free to spend as much time as you like with him." He paused, then took a deep breath. "I hear you had a bit of excitement earlier," he said. "Ghyllie tells me you saved the day."

Samantha shrugged, keeping her attention on Finn, who had turned his back so that she could scratch his rump. "It wasn't really that big a deal," she said. "I hope you're not upset with me for risking Colm by racing him like that."

"Not a bit," Jimmy said, leaning his forearms on the fence. "The truth of the matter is, I'd like to see you do some riding myself. Maybe tomorrow we can set up the arena with a few jumps, and you can show me what you know."

"That would be fun," Samantha said. "I'm looking forward to it."

True to his word, Jimmy had the large outdoor arena prepared the next morning. The sun was shining, giving the green fields a depth of color that made

Samantha understand why Ireland was called the Emerald Isle. Since there were no other visitors scheduled for the day, Ghyllian joined them, impressing Samantha with her skill over the jumps Jimmy had set up.

"Well," Jimmy said as Samantha rode a silver mare named Fey Sprite to the fence, "you were serious when you said you knew a bit about riding." He turned to watch Tor take Night Sky over a five-foot brush wall and nodded in approval. "The two of you are free to ride any horse on the place," he said. "It's truly a pleasure to have a pair of fine horse people like yourself on the farm."

"Mum packed us a lunch to take," Ghyllian announced, leading her bay mare, Bridget, to the fence. "I thought we could take my favorite trail and go up on the bluffs that overlook the sea."

"That sounds great," Samantha said. Soon she and Tor were following Ghyllian along the road, and Samantha couldn't take in enough of the scenery, trying to absorb everything at once.

"A month isn't going to be long enough," she told Tor as they rode past a cluster of stone cottages. A woman sat in the sun in front of one cottage, her foot busily pumping the treadle of a spinning wheel, and in the field behind the house, a group of children were riding Connemara ponies. They waved and called out as the Nelsons rode by, and Samantha smiled and waved back.

Ghyllian led them up a rough trail to the bluffs, where they ate their lunch near the ruins of an old stone cottage overlooking the Irish Sea. Samantha sighed contentedly, gazing out across the lichen-coated rocks to the sunlight glinting off the water's surface. "This is just incredible," she murmured. When they climbed back on their horses to return to Celtic Meadows, she hung back, hating to leave the rugged beauty of the coast, but there was so much more to do.

"I could stay here forever," she told Tor one day while they were visiting Finn in his turnout. Kerry Maid was rubbing her chin on Tor's shoulder while Samantha slipped a halter over Finn's muzzle, letting him get used to its feel. When she asked him to step forward, the colt moved toward her without any hesitation, and before long she was leading him around the paddock as if he'd always been halter-broken.

Tor and Samantha rode every day, sometimes

with Ghyllian over some challenging cross-country courses she showed them, and sometimes in the arena, working with the Hollises' horses. When they weren't in the saddle, Samantha spent her free time with Finn, working with the colt every day.

"I wish we didn't have to leave yet!" Samantha exclaimed the day their flight was scheduled to leave. She and Tor were in their room, packing their clothing and souvenirs for the trip home.

"No?" Tor asked.

"We never got to see any steeplechases," Samantha said, carefully folding the hand-knit sweater Tor had bought her and laying it in her suitcase. "We need at least another month."

"Maybe we'll come back in a few years," Tor said with a hopeful smile. "We can watch Finn race in the Grand National."

Samantha sighed. "I'm going to miss him most of all," she said, wondering if she would ever see the colt again.

Ghyllian rode to the airport with them, and before Samantha and Tor went through the gate to their plane, she gave Samantha a tearful hug good-bye.

"Don't forget me," she said. "I'm going to miss you both so much."

"We'll miss you, too," Samantha promised. She blinked back her own tears as they climbed aboard the plane and settled into their seats for the long flight home.

4

SAMANTHA RESTED HER ELBOWS ON THE FENCE RAIL AND gazed across the white-fenced meadows surrounding Whisperwood. A cool breeze stirred the late autumn air, rippling across the grass. Samantha sighed, watching Miss Battleship and Shining graze in their turnouts. The month in Ireland seemed like a long-past dream. In spite of how busy she and Tor were at Whisperwood, in quiet moments like this Samantha found herself lost in thought, recalling the days at Celtic Meadows. She missed riding through the countryside with Tor, eating Hannah's cooking in the cozy kitchen, and visiting with Jimmy and Ghyllian. But more than anything, she missed the time she had spent with Finn.

Miss Battleship lifted her head and gazed at Samantha with mild interest, then turned back to the grass underfoot, but Shining ambled to the fence, nudging Samantha with her copper-colored nose.

Get over it, Samantha ordered herself, petting Shining. *It was a nice vacation, but this is home. This spring we'll breed Miss Battleship to a stallion, maybe Jazzman, and before long Tor and I will be busy training our own home-bred steeplechasers.*

Samantha stroked Shining's glossy flank. Mandy Jarvis, one of their riding students, had come to Whisperwood daily to spend time with the mare while Samantha and Tor were gone, so Samantha knew that her beloved Thoroughbred had received plenty of attention.

As much as she tried to settle back into life in Kentucky, Samantha felt like she had left a part of herself in Ireland. She couldn't get past the longing she felt to go back, ride across the countryside, and listen to the colorful stories Jimmy had told in the evenings about his experiences on the Irish racetracks. He had a knack for storytelling, sharing Irish lore, legends, and, as Hannah described them, "a few tall tales of his own creation." Samantha could still hear Jimmy's rich brogue as he said, "Hannah, love, you know the best part of the story is in the telling, not the truth of it." Samantha smiled at the memory. She and Tor had laughed until their sides ached, while Hannah and Ghyllian had rolled their eyes and shook their heads in dismay.

"You look completely lost in thought," Tor said, startling Samantha out of her reverie.

"I was just thinking about Ireland," she admitted, turning to smile at her husband.

Tor had his hands shoved deep in the pockets of his worn barn jacket, and he leaned close to plant a light kiss on Samantha's forehead. "You miss it a lot, don't you?" he asked, looking out across the field.

"I shouldn't feel homesick for a place I only visited for a short time," Samantha admitted. She wrinkled her nose. "I mean, it *is* nice to be home with our own horses."

Tor nodded. "I know how you feel," he said. "I miss Ireland, too. But," he continued, "we have a great life here, and we can plan another vacation at Celtic Meadows for an anniversary, right?" He reached over and patted Shining's neck.

Samantha gazed up at him. "Of course," she said. But another trip wasn't what she really longed for. The four weeks had gone by so quickly that it seemed like four years wouldn't be enough time to spend in Ireland.

When she saw the attention Shining was getting at the fence, Miss Battleship walked to the corner of her turnout and nudged Tor's hand with her red-brown nose. He stroked the mare's shoulder. "I'm looking forward to breeding her and seeing what kind of foals she gives us."

"Me too," Samantha said.

"Thanksgiving is only a few weeks away," Tor said, rubbing Miss Battleship's forehead. "And after that, Christmas. Then we'll be busy with new foals and spring breeding season."

"I know," Samantha said, reaching over to scratch Miss Battleship's poll. "I've been happy working with Sierra and helping with lessons. I do love it here."

"But your heart is somewhere else," Tor said, giving her a knowing look.

Samantha smiled. "Only part of it," she said. "The best part of it is with you, wherever you are." She gave her head a quick shake. "I'm sure what I miss most is that we had such a good time. I know Gregg and Yvonne want to go back to Italy after the great honeymoon they had there. That's all it is for me, too." She reached up to pat Tor's cheek softly. "I'm fine, really."

"Speaking of the Dohertys, we need to get together with them for dinner soon," Tor said. Gregg and Yvonne, their close friends, had gotten married the year before Samantha and Tor. The couples tried to get together regularly, aside from the work they did together with the Pony Commandos, the handicapped riding group Tor had helped start years before.

"I'll call Yvonne this evening," Samantha promised.

"I need to set up the indoor arena for lessons," Tor said. "Do you want to give me a hand?"

"Sure," Samantha said, eager to be busy at something to keep her mind off Ireland. "After lessons maybe we can take Top Hat and Sierra out for a short ride."

"It's a plan," Tor said, hooking his arm around her waist. "Now let's get back to work."

The weeks sped by, and as Christmas approached, Ashleigh invited Samantha to go into Lexington to finish their Christmas shopping. They drove along the cheerfully decorated streets, with holiday ornaments and colorful lights hanging from the light poles and covering the storefronts.

"I want to go to the tack store first," Ashleigh said.

"Of course," Samantha replied, gazing out the car window at the festive shop windows. "I want to get Tor a new barn jacket. His old one is completely worn out."

They went from store to store, and Samantha found gifts for Cindy, her brother, Kevin, Beth, her stepmother, and her father, then spotted a stuffed chestnut pony that looked perfect for Christina. After paying for her selections, she turned to Ashleigh. "I'm starving," she announced. "How can shopping make me so hungry?"

Ashleigh nodded, her own arms loaded with the gifts she had purchased. "I don't know, but I'm hungry, too," she said. "Let's put this stuff in the car and find a restaurant."

When they went into a cozy diner on a downtown street corner, Samantha inhaled deeply. "That smells like Hannah's beef stew," she said. "I know what I'm having for lunch."

They found seats in a booth, and Ashleigh eyed Samantha from across the table. "You still miss it, don't you?"

Samantha grimaced. "Am I that obvious?" she asked.

Ashleigh nodded. "I can tell you're thinking

about Ireland by the look in your eyes," she said. "You get a faraway expression, and you sigh a lot."

"You make it sound so dopey," Samantha said, taking a drink of water from the glass the waitress had set in front of her.

"No," Ashleigh said, "it isn't the least bit silly. You had a wonderful time there."

"And now we're going to have a great life right here," Samantha replied firmly.

When the waitress returned, Samantha ordered the stew, but she was disappointed when it didn't seem to have the same flavor as Hannah's cooking. She was sure what she was missing wasn't the quality of the food, but eating in the kitchen with the Hollis family, sharing stories and making plans for the next day's activities.

When they left the restaurant, Ashleigh drove them to the mall to finish their shopping. Samantha found a white wool fisherman's sweater for Tor and a coffee cup with a shamrock design on it for Tor's father.

"I'm sure they'll love those," Ashleigh said, picking up a silk scarf to send to her older sister, Caroline, who was living out of the country with her husband.

It was dusk by the time they drove back to Whisperwood. The lights from the ranch house spilled out the windows in a golden glow as they pulled up the driveway. Samantha saw Mike's pickup parked in front of the house alongside Beth's sedan.

"It looks like there's a party going on," Ashleigh said, climbing from the car. Samantha followed her, lugging her shopping bags, and when Tor opened the door for them, she felt warmed by the broad smile on his face.

"Welcome home, shoppers," he said cheerfully. "Dad called over to Whitebrook and invited the families to get together for the evening. And now that you two are here, the festivities can begin."

Samantha was sure that Tor was worried that she wasn't happy at Whisperwood, and she felt selfish about the way she had been moping. *I'm going to be more grateful about what a wonderful life I have,* she told herself, setting her bags down so that she could wrap her arms around Tor's neck. "Thank you," she murmured, pressing her face against his warm neck.

"It's the holiday season," he said. "What could be better than having a little get-together?"

After a dinner of Mr. Nelson's lasagna, Mike's homemade bread, and a salad Beth had put together, they settled in the living room to listen to music and visit. Christina and Kevin lay on the floor watching cartoons, and Samantha nestled next to Tor on the sofa.

"Is Cindy coming home for Christmas?" she asked her father.

Ian shook his head. "I don't think so," he said. "She's going a mile a minute up in New York, trying to make a life for herself." Samantha's younger sister had followed her own dream, moving first to Dubai and then to New York to try to establish herself as a professional jockey. Her new life kept her busy, and she hadn't had a lot of contact with the family since her move.

Samantha nodded thoughtfully. "She's doing exactly what she wants," she said. "I'm glad for her."

"We're happy for her, too," Ian replied. "But we miss her anyway."

The phone rang, and Tor went into the kitchen to answer it. He was gone for several minutes, and when he returned to the living room, he had a dazed look on his face.

"What is it?" Samantha asked, jumping up from the sofa.

Tor's expression was serious, but his eyes were bright. "You're not going to believe this," he said. "That was Jimmy Hollis, Sammy."

"Is everything all right?" she asked. "Are Hannah and Ghyllian okay? Did something happen to Finn?"

Tor shook his head. "Things are going really well for them. They've decided to close the bed-and-breakfast."

"Oh, no!" Samantha exclaimed. "Where will we stay when we go back?"

"They're in the process of expanding the farm," Tor went on, "building new barns, and Jimmy is going to spend more time on breeding flat-track race-horses. He wants to raise a colt that will run in the Kentucky Derby someday."

"That's wonderful, but where will we stay?" Samantha asked again.

"That's why he called," Tor replied. "He asked if you and I would be interested in moving to Ireland to run the eventing part of the farm. How does that sound to you?"

Samantha felt her jaw drop, and she stared at Tor in disbelief. "Go to work in Ireland?"

"How exciting!" Beth exclaimed, clapping her hands together.

"This is the chance of a lifetime for you two," Mr. Nelson said, a broad smile stretching across his face.

"But we have so much work here," Samantha

protested, looking from Tor's father to Ian. "We can't leave Whisperwood."

"Oh, yes, you can," Mr. Nelson said firmly. "This is a great opportunity for both of you, and if it's what you want, you have to go for it."

"What about our horses here?" Samantha asked. "What would I do with Shining?"

"We'll get it all figured out," Ashleigh said. "The Jarvises would love to have her, you know that."

Samantha knew Ashleigh was right. Mandy adored the mare and had helped Samantha turn her into a good saddle horse after the veterinarian had recommended against breeding her again. Samantha looked back to Tor, thrilled to see the excitement in his face.

"Think of it, Sammy," he said. "We'd be working with Irish steeplechasers, training and riding against the toughest competition in the world."

Samantha turned to her father, and her heart soared when she saw the pleased look on his face. "You'd all be okay with us living in another country?" she asked him. "I know it's hard for you with Cindy gone, and she isn't that far away."

Ian rose and crossed the room to give her a hug. "If it's what you want, then go for it," he said. "Of course we'll miss you, but this is such a great opportunity. Don't let anyone here hold you back."

Samantha looked into Tor's face. "What did you tell Jimmy?" she asked.

"I told him I'd talk it over with my wife and get back to him," Tor said. "I was pretty sure what your answer would be, but now I know for certain. I'll give him a call back, and we can start making the necessary arrangements."

"This means I'll get to work with Finn every day," Samantha said, feeling her heart soar. She looked around at the family and friends gathered in the living room. "Thank you all for being so supportive about this," she said.

"We're excited for you," Beth said warmly. "You're going to live in Ireland and work with Irish hunters, Samantha. How could we not be happy about it?"

When Beth's words sank in, the reality of what had just happened hit Samantha, and she threw her arms around Tor's neck. "We're really doing it," she exclaimed. "We're going back to Ireland!"

5

IT WAS THE END OF FEBRUARY BEFORE ALL THE DETAILS WERE taken care of and Samantha and Tor could leave for their new jobs in Ireland.

"Are we doing the right thing?" she asked Tor the day the Jarvis family came to take Shining away. She had the chestnut mare in the crossties, running a soft rag along Shining's sleek coat. The mare nuzzled Samantha's shoulder, and Samantha paused to caress Shining's neck.

Tor leaned against the barn wall, his arms folded in front of him. "Yes," he said firmly. "Shining will be happy with Mandy. You know that, Sammy."

Samantha sighed and nodded. "I'm going to miss

her," she said. "What if things don't work out with the Jarvises?"

But when Mandy and her parents came into the barn, Shining nickered at the girl, who hurried up the aisle, a new halter in her hands, her face glowing with excitement. She held out the halter for Shining to smell, and looked at Samantha, her eyes bright. "I'm going give her the best care in the world," she said. "I'll send you tons of pictures and letters." Shining snuffled at Mandy's curly dark hair, sighing contentedly, and Samantha felt her worries about the mare slip away.

"Thanks, Mandy," she said, giving the girl's shoulders a squeeze. She helped Mandy put Shining in the horse trailer, giving the horse a good-bye hug before she stepped out of the trailer and shut the door.

"Everything is working out perfectly," Tor said as they watched the Jarvises drive away. "Now we need to finish packing and get ourselves ready to leave."

"Oh, Tor," Samantha said, gripping his arm as they stepped off the plane. "We're really back in Ireland to stay. After all the planning and work we've done to make it happen, I can hardly believe we're really here."

Tor looked at her, a broad smile stretched across his face. "It doesn't seem real, does it?" he asked, then looked around the terminal for a familiar face.

"Over here!" Ghyllian was standing near the luggage carousel, waving at them. Samantha and Tor hurried over to her, and Ghyllian threw her arms around Samantha, giving her a warm, welcoming hug. "I'm so happy to see you two!" she exclaimed. "Let's get your bags and head for Celtic Meadows. You won't believe how much has changed since last summer."

They followed Ghyllian to the parking lot and soon were headed away from the airport and toward Celtic Meadows. The misty rain that had been falling when they arrived stopped as they drove south. A bright rainbow arched across the blue sky, and the spring sunlight made the wet fields glisten. Samantha pointed at the rainbow. "How perfect," she exclaimed.

"It looks to me like Ireland is welcoming you home," Ghyllian said with a grin.

Samantha sighed happily, watching the now familiar landscape pass as they drove through the countryside. "How's my boy Finn?" she asked Ghyllian.

"He's huge," Ghyllian said. "And sweet as can be. I know he's going to be glad to see you."

When they pulled up to the stone house, Samantha hopped from the car and looked around. A new stable had been erected near the long building that housed the jumpers, and a white-painted railing enclosed a small practice track for the racehorses.

"Your dad's done a lot," Tor commented, pressing his hands to the small of his back and stretching as he looked around at the changes to the farm.

"He's been busy," Ghyllian agreed. "He wanted to wait for the two of you to get here before he does anything with the eventing facilities, so he put all his attention on setting things up for the racehorses." She tipped her head toward the new barn. "Let's go see the new stock," she said. "Mum's dashing about the house trying to get a lovely meal put together, so we'll give her a bit more time before we bother her."

Tor and Samantha followed Ghyllian to the big stable, and Samantha walked through the doorway, stopping to take in the long, wide aisle lined with roomy box stalls. In the stall nearest the door, a tall bay horse stuck his nose over the door and snorted loudly.

"That's Juniper," Ghyllian said, holding her hand

out so that the colt could sniff her palm. "He's the newest Thoroughbred Dad's bought. We'll be racing him at Curragh in Kildare in the spring. They have a grand flat track there."

"He's a good-looking fellow," Samantha commented, eyeing the colt's long neck and elegant head.

"He's got a knack for coming out of the gate fast and holding his pace for the distance," Ghyllian said. "Dad's really pleased with him."

Farther down the aisle, an athletic-looking chestnut colt swiveled his ears and eyed the trio as they approached his stall. "Who's this?" Tor asked, gazing at the big red-brown horse.

"Alybain," Ghyllian said. "He's got some dynamite bloodlines, like Alydar and Affirmed. Dad's got big plans for him."

"Hello!"

Samantha and Tor turned to see Jimmy striding down the aisle, smiling warmly at them. "Good to have you back," the farm owner said, slapping Tor on the back, then turning to Samantha, his arms open wide. He gave her a hug, then held her at arm's length. "I don't know how it could be, but you've grown even more beautiful," he said. "That hair of yours glows like the sky at sundown, and those green eyes sparkle like emeralds. You could light up a room just by walking into it, darlin'."

Samantha felt herself blush at the blatant flattery. "And your gift of blarney is as impressive as ever," she said with a laugh. "It's so good to see you, Jimmy."

"I'm sure you're wanting to see Finn," Jimmy said.

"You know I do," Samantha said.

"He's going to be your special project," Jimmy said. "And you'll want to inspect the new facilities to see if they're up to your standards."

Tor looked around the barn and chuckled. "You couldn't have done any better, Jimmy," he said. "Everything looks great."

"I'm glad you think so," Jimmy said. "Let's finish the tour and get up to the house." Samantha and Tor fell in step beside him as he headed for the barn door.

When they rounded the corner of the barn, Samantha gave a little gasp. The massive brown colt standing in the turnout beside the eventing horses' stable couldn't possibly be Finn.

"He grew!" she said, gaping at the colt. At the sound of her voice, Finn snapped his head in their direction. He gave a welcoming nicker, and trotted to the fence, testing the air to catch Samantha's scent. He whinnied loudly, stretching his neck over the fence.

Samantha hurried over to him, and the colt lipped at her hair, blowing warm air against her neck.

"Finn," she crooned, stroking his muscular shoulder. "You are a giant!"

"He's barely a year," Jimmy said. "Imagine what he's going to be like when he's two."

"Awesome," Tor murmured. He walked up to the fence and patted the colt's nose. "He sure is glad to see you," he said to Samantha.

Samantha looked at Tor and shook her head. "Isn't he something to see?" she asked. "He's going to devour the competition in a couple of years, aren't you, boy?"

Finn snorted and tossed his head, then wheeled away from the fence and pranced off in a stiff-legged gait that had Samantha chuckling. "What a show-off," she said fondly.

"I guess we'd best get to the house now," Jimmy said. "We've got business to sort out, and I expect Hannah has supper ready. Now that she isn't feeding the tourists, she's trying to fatten Ghyllian and me up. It's a good thing the two of you are here to help us eat all her cooking."

They strolled back past the new barn, stopping at

the car to pick up the luggage, then went into the farmhouse. Samantha inhaled deeply, taking in the comforting, familiar smells that filled the kitchen.

"Welcome back!" Hannah said, meeting them at the door. She flung her arms around Samantha, then Tor, giving them each a hug. "I was just getting ready to hunt you four down at the barn," she said, untying her apron. "Now have a seat and we'll get a bite of food in you." She frowned at Samantha. "I think you've lost a bit of weight since you were here."

"Only what I gained last summer," Samantha said, laughing.

"Now," Jimmy said when they were seated at the table, "I know you'll be wanting a little place of your own instead of staying in this old hovel of ours, so we've taken it upon ourselves to fix up the old care-taker's cottage."

"That cute little house on the other side of the field?" Tor asked, spreading butter on a piece of Hannah's fresh bread.

"That would be it," Jimmy said. "It's a wee bit small, but it should be about right for the two of you. Of course," he added, "you're welcome to find a place on your own, but that'll be a good starting point for you."

"Thank you," Samantha said, touched by the Hol-

Abingdon Elementary School Library
Abingdon, Virginia

lises' thoughtfulness. "I think it'll be perfect, and it's close to the barns."

"It's fully furnished," Hannah said. "Nothing too fancy, but it does make a cozy little place to lay your head at night, and you can start the day off with a cup of tea on the stoop."

After they had finished eating and made plans for the next day's chores, Ghyllian drove them down to the cottage. She pointed at an old pickup parked outside the door. "That's for your use," she told them as she helped unload their suitcases from the car. "You'll have to get used to driving on the opposite side of the road, but I'm sure you'll figure it out in short order."

When they walked inside the cottage, Samantha clapped her hands together in delight. "This is wonderful," she said, looking at the lacy curtains that hung at the windows, and the sturdy table and chairs in the kitchen. A bouquet of fresh flowers sat in the middle of the table. In the living room, a colorful throw covered the sofa, brightening the small room.

"Mum stocked up some food for you," Ghyllian informed them, opening the kitchen cupboards to show the boxes of crackers, canned foods, and a tin of tea. "Your own teapot," she said with a grin, holding up a pan.

"Great," Samantha said. "Ever since last summer, I've drunk way more tea than coffee."

Ghyllian showed them the tiny bathroom, and Tor set their suitcases inside the door of the cottage's small bedroom.

"I'll leave you be," Ghyllian said. "If there's anything you're wanting, just let me know."

"I think we'll be very happy here," Samantha said. "We'll see you first thing in the morning at the barn."

After Ghyllian left, Samantha strolled through the house, peering out each of the windows. From the kitchen she could see the paddocks and the back of the older barn, and a short distance from that, the main house. When she went into the living room, Tor was on the sofa, his legs stretched out and his hands clasped behind his head.

"It's been quite a day, hasn't it?" Samantha asked him.

Tor yawned, then rubbed his eyes. "And it's just going to get better from here," he said. "Right now we'd better get some sleep. Starting tomorrow, we're going to be pretty busy."

Tor was still sleeping soundly when Samantha awoke early the next morning. The first thing she did was to fix a cup of tea in the little kitchen. She wrapped a blanket around her shoulders and, the mug of steaming brew in hand, stepped outside, wiggling her bare toes on the cold stone step in front of the door. "I need to get a good pair of wool slippers," she said to herself. She inhaled the sweet scent of the tea and looked across the mist-shrouded fields toward the barns. "Welcome home, Samantha," she murmured, sighing happily.

She knew she would miss the people and horses they had left behind, but at that moment, with everything so new and exciting, it was impossible to feel homesick for Kentucky.

"Hey," Tor said, leaning out the cottage door. "Do you want some breakfast to go with that tea? We're wasting daylight, Mrs. Nelson."

"I'll be right in," Samantha promised. "I know we have a lot to do."

An hour later they met Jimmy at his office in the racehorse barn. "Top of the morning to you both," he greeted them, gesturing at a pair of folding chairs across from his desk. "I was just going through the lists of things I'd like done. But first," he said, "I'd like you both to visit a couple of other farms with me. You can see how they're handling their facilities and meet a few of the other farm managers."

He looked at Samantha. "After watching how you were with Finn last summer," he said. "I want you to work with him and a couple of the other yearlings I've got that are my steeplechase prospects. I'll have John, the groom, introduce you to the broodmares. We expect to have some nice foals again this year, and you'll be handling them from the start."

"That sounds great to me," Samantha said, eager to start working closely with the young horses.

Jimmy turned to Tor. "You'll be working with the older horses," he said. "From what I've seen of your riding, you're a good, aggressive jockey. Once you've gotten settled here, I'd like you to ride in a few chases for me."

"I'd love that," Tor said.

"Then of course there's always other work to do around here," Jimmy said, waving his hand to encompass the farm. "I'm sure you'll find plenty to keep yourselves busy."

After Jimmy had taken them to tour some of the neighboring farms and introduced them to some of the local horse people, he and Tor sat down to go through the training schedules for the jumpers, and Samantha went out to Finn's pasture. The big colt came up to the fence to greet her, and Samantha let herself into the field, pausing to scratch his neck before she slipped a halter over his head. "We're going to have a great time together," she told him, leading the colt out of the pasture. "Let's get you groomed, and then we'll spend a little time in the round pen."

Samantha was amazed at how quickly Finn picked up on her cues, and by the time she was done with his short training session, she knew he was going to be the best horse she had ever had the chance to work with.

That evening, when they returned to the cottage, they sat down at their kitchen table to review the day and eat the casserole Hannah had sent home with them. As darkness settled over the farm Samantha turned on a lamp in the cozy living room, then turned to Tor, happy to see a contented smile on his face. Tor crossed the room and swept her into his arms. "Life is good," he said.

"We're living in an honest-to-goodness Irish cottage," Samantha told him. "It's like a dream come true."

"The work is real enough," Tor reminded her.

"But it's what we love," Samantha replied.

"First thing tomorrow, I'm taking one of the three-year-olds over a cross-country course. I told Jimmy I'd like both of us to do some three-day eventing with a couple of the younger horses and get a feel for how they go before we try any Irish steeplechases."

"Wonderful!" Samantha exclaimed in delight. "Three-day eventing in Ireland. How much better can things get?"

"The competition is going to be tough," Tor reminded her.

"And it's going to force us both to become even better riders," Samantha said. "This is all so amazing. Not only do I get to train the most talented colt in the world, I'm really going to be competing on horseback in Ireland. I feel like the luckiest person in the world."

Tor gave her a warm smile. "Then I'm going to stick close to you," he teased her. "That way maybe more of your Irish luck will rub off on me."

6

TOR AND SAMANTHA SETTLED INTO A COMFORTABLE routine, working with the eventing horses and making friends in the community. Every morning when she woke up, Samantha looked around the cottage, feeling as though she was living the greatest dream in the world. The days slipped by in a happy blur. While Tor began steeplechasing regularly, Samantha geared Finn toward event riding, with Jimmy's approval.

"It'll be good training for when he starts racing," he told Samantha after watching her take the colt over a tall brush jump one spring morning. "Just don't turn him into a prissy show pony."

"Like there's any chance of that," Samantha said,

patting Finn's muscular shoulder. "Prissy doesn't suit him at all!"

"Finn is the easiest horse I've ever trained," she told Ghyllian one day while they were grooming the colt in preparation for a small event at one of the local farms.

"He won't be competing in these little events for long," Ghyllian predicted. "You can just tell by looking at him that the two of you are going to go places."

"I can't believe we're really here, Finn," Samantha said, stepping inside Jimmy's horse trailer. "It doesn't seem possible that we're competing in the Badminton Horse Trials."

All around them in the parking area of the duke of Beaufort's home in Gloucestershire, England, the impatient stamping of feet, loud, excited whinnies from the other horses, and the voices of grooms, trainers, and riders filled the spring air. Four-year-old Finn pawed at the trailer floor, eager to get out. He whinnied, the sound ringing in the trailer, and Samantha pressed her hands to her ears.

"Now everyone in the United Kingdom knows you're here, boy," she said, patting his sleek brown neck. She unclipped the trailer tie and led the horse out the door, where Finn stopped abruptly, his large body tense, his ears pointed and his muscular neck arched as he looked around.

"He is so handsome," Ghyllian said, propping her hands on her hips as she eyed the excited horse.

"And he knows it," Samantha said, running her hand along Finn's nose. He flared his nostrils and inhaled deeply, taking in the strange scents, prancing in place.

"We finally get to show the whole world what we've managed to accomplish in the last few years," Samantha said.

"You've already had tons of press coverage," Ghyllian pointed out. "The horse world is well aware of Finn and you."

Samantha had a scrapbook full of photos of the horse and her, along with articles detailing their wins and successes on the three-day eventing circuit. But still, she wondered if she and Finn were really good enough to ride against the Olympic-class equestrians there for the trials. *Skill and hard work got you this far,* she reminded herself. *Now isn't the time to have any doubts.*

She gazed around at the mix of people unloading

their world-class horses in the back lot. She knew most of the horses and riders from events in which she and Finn had competed, as well as from the televised coverage of events from around the world.

"I'll take Finn to Badminton House for his checkup," Ghyllian said. "There are already quite a few horses there, and I don't want to be last in line."

"Thanks," Samantha said, giving the horse a pat before handing his lead to the girl. She watched Ghyllian and Finn head for the stone mansion, owned by the duke of Beaufort, whose family sponsored the world-renowned event.

Samantha turned and opened the storage compartment of the trailer to pull out her duffel bag. A photo fell out of a side pocket and fluttered to the ground. Samantha bent over to pick it up, pausing to look at the picture before she tucked it back into the bag.

The snapshot of her father, Beth, and Kevin had been taken in front of their cottage at Whitebrook the previous Christmas. Samantha carried it with her whenever she was competing because it made her feel a little as though her family were close by. She gazed at the familiar faces, trying to imagine what Kevin was like at the age of nine. Although they talked on the phone every week, she felt like she hardly knew her little brother.

It didn't seem possible that it had been over three years since their move to Ireland. The time had flown by, and she and Tor were busy every day with the eventing program at Celtic Meadows, training the jumpers, working with the steeplechasers, and, for Samantha, pouring every spare moment she had into working with Finn.

As Jimmy got more involved with his flat-track racers, he had given them full control of the eventing facility, from purchasing horses to hiring the stable hands they needed as they expanded. Samantha knew the experience of running the facility was invaluable if they ever wanted to run their own farm, but sometimes it seemed as though they were too busy. *We're doing what we love*, she reminded herself. *Not everyone can say that about their work.*

"Sammy!" Samantha's friend Molly Flynn strode up to her, smiling brightly. Jimmy had introduced Samantha and Tor to the petite brunette and her husband, Joe, during their first few weeks in Ireland, and the four had quickly become close friends. Joe, a veteran steeplechase jockey, had shared everything he knew about Irish steeplechasing with Tor and Samantha, helping them prepare for the rigors of riding against the tough competition on the Irish tracks. Molly, a schoolteacher, didn't ride competitively, but she often went on hacks with Samantha, helping her exercise the jumpers. As a representative for the Equestrian Federation of Ireland, Joe was one of the officials working at the horse trials that year.

"Are you ready for this?" Molly asked, indicating the throng of competitors and their horses.

"I'm nervous as a cat in a room full of rocking chairs," Samantha replied, only half joking.

"You still plan to go to the ball tonight, don't you?" Molly asked. "That'll help you unwind a bit before your dressage test tomorrow."

"I wouldn't miss the party for anything," Samantha said. "It sounds like it's going to be a great time, and I bought the most perfect dress to wear."

"It'll be a grand evening," Molly said.

"I'd better go sign in," Samantha said. She smiled at her friend. "Then I need to get Finn settled in his stall before we head for the hotel."

"I'm supposed to meet Joe at Badminton House," Molly said. "I'll see you tonight." Molly headed across the parking area toward the massive house, and Samantha joined the line of competitors checking in at the event officials' booth. After a long wait, she finally got her papers turned in. She took her information packet and number and crossed the stable courtyard to Finn's stall.

Ghyllian and Tor already had the horse put up. The stall was padded with thick bedding, and Tor was filling Finn's hay net while Ghyllian topped off his water bucket. Finn had his head stuck over the half door, looking around curiously.

"He's happy," Tor announced, hanging the hay net inside the stall door.

"What a sweet boy," Samantha said, giving the horse's shiny nose a pet. Finn bobbed his head vigorously as if in agreement, and Samantha laughed, stroking his neck fondly. "This is going to be a great weekend," she told the horse. "You get to show off what you can do, and I'll try my best to help you along."

"You'll do an excellent job," Tor said. "Both of you are outstanding. You wouldn't be here if you weren't a winning team."

"Finn just comes alive when you're riding him, Sammy," Ghyllian said. "You two are going to put on a performance people will talk about for a long time."

"I only hope he behaves himself during the dressage test tomorrow," Samantha said. "He can be such a grump about dressage work. He'd much rather be running and jumping."

"His points in the stadium jumping and cross-country more than make up for the dressage tests," Ghyllian said. "And it isn't that he doesn't perform dressage well. He just enjoys the other things so much more."

"We'd better get to the hotel," Tor said, glancing at his watch. "It's getting late, and we need to get ready for the ball."

"Dad and Mum should be at their rooms by now, too," Ghyllian said. "I need to get with them, and we'll see you at the ball."

That evening Samantha stood in front of the bathroom mirror in their hotel room, debating whether or not to put her hair up. She hated to fuss with her appearance, but finally she swept it up and pinned it in place, wanting to show off the emerald necklace Tor had given her for her birthday. The halter top of her gold taffeta gown exposed her shoulders, and the full skirt of the dress rustled softly as she moved.

"Can you close the clasp on this bracelet for me?" she asked Tor, coming out of the bathroom.

Tor looked up from buttoning his jacket and smiled. "You're gorgeous," he said. "I'm going to have the most beautiful woman in Ireland on my arm tonight. I don't think anyone at the ball will be able to keep their eyes off you."

"And I'll be with the most handsome man," she replied, holding out the bracelet. Tor carefully closed the clasp of the glistening emeralds and sapphires around her wrist.

"That was your mom's, wasn't it?" he asked. "The last time you wore it was when we got married."

Samantha nodded, running a finger over the delicate bracelet. "Dad gave it to me at our wedding," she said, thinking back to their wonderful horseback wedding at Whitebrook. She smiled at Tor. "That was such an incredible day," she said. "And our lives have gotten better every day since."

"It's that Irish luck you bring to us," Tor said, grimacing as he struggled to fasten his bow tie.

Samantha reached up and expertly tied the bow, then stepped back and ran her hands down the front of Tor's black jacket. "You do look fabulous in a tuxedo, Mr. Nelson," she said.

"Are you ready to go?" Tor asked. "We're supposed to be there at eight o'clock sharp for the reception." He held out his arm, and Samantha tucked her hand around the crook of his elbow. They left their room and headed for the elevator down to the ballroom.

The hall was filling up with guests when they arrived, and Samantha spotted Molly and Joe standing with a group of people across the room. She recognized Mark Todd, the New Zealand rider who had won the horse trials twice, and Captain Mark Phillips, the British eventing winner who had gone on to become a highly successful trainer. Samantha looked around the room, seeing several other well-known competitors and coaches, and felt a shiver. She was definitely out of her league around these people.

"I'm going to grab a glass of punch," Tor said. "Can I bring you one?"

"Not right now," Samantha said. "I'm going to say hello to Joe and Molly." Tor left for the refreshment table, and Samantha was just about to start across the room when a touch on her arm stopped her.

"Mrs. Nelson?"

Samantha turned to see a woman in a long black

dress, a press pass on her sequined jacket, holding a notepad and small tape recorder. "I'm Nora Carroll," she said in a thick Irish brogue. "I write for *International Sport Horse News*, and wondered if I could chat you up a bit. Mr. Hollis said you'd be happy to talk with me."

Samantha looked around the room, filled with dozens of the top riders in the world, and saw Jimmy and Hannah standing with Ghyllian and a group of other owners. Jimmy smiled and waved to her, and Samantha waved back, then turned to Nora and raised her eyebrows. "With all these famous riders to choose from, you want to talk to me?"

Nora smiled. "You've built quite a reputation," she said. "You and Finn McCoul are fast becoming household names around here."

"What would you like to know?" Samantha asked.

"Tell me how you got involved with horses," Nora urged her.

Samantha quickly reviewed her years of growing up around the Thoroughbred racetracks on the East Coast until her father took the job of head trainer at Whitebrook.

"Whitebrook," Nora repeated. "So you've spent

years around some rather famous horses, like Ashleigh's Wonder, Wonder's Champion, and Wonder's Pride."

"That's right," Samantha said, smiling to herself as she thought about the outstanding Thoroughbreds she had worked with.

"It's no surprise, then, that you're such a talented horsewoman yourself," Nora said. "And I've seen your husband race in a couple of chases at Punchestown. He's quite a capable jockey."

"He's a good coach as well," Samantha replied. "He's taught me everything I know about jumping."

"You're lucky to have such a helpful partner," Nora said. "I'll look forward to seeing you compete this weekend."

Nora walked off in search of another rider to interview, and Samantha hurried across the room to where Tor was visiting with Molly and Joe.

"An interview with Nora Carroll makes you pretty exclusive," Joe said, raising his glass in a toast to Samantha. "Here's to a successful weekend for Finn and you."

As the group raised their glasses, Samantha smiled, grateful for the support and encouragement of her friends.

When Samantha rose the next morning, the weather was perfect for the day's events, clear and mild. When she and Tor got to Finn's stall, the horse greeted them with a loud whinny, shoving his nose against Samantha's chest, demanding attention.

"He's putting in his order for breakfast," she said, rubbing his poll.

"I'll get right on it, sir," Tor said, giving the horse a pat on the neck before he headed for the storage room to mix Finn's grain and fill his hay net. While Finn enjoyed his breakfast, Samantha and Tor reviewed the schedule for the weekend. "Your dressage test is at eleven-thirty," Tor said. "Tomorrow you're number six to ride the cross-country course. Then, if you're one of the top twenty, you'll be in the stadium jumping rounds."

"I'm here to groom your horse," Ghyllian announced when she showed up at the stall an hour later. "We want him to look the picture of perfection for the judges."

"I'd better go get myself together," Samantha said, giving Tor a kiss before she headed for the dressing rooms. She took her time getting into her show clothes, making sure her hair was well secured under her helmet. Her tall boots were polished to a deep shine, and the gold buttons on her jacket gleamed.

When she returned to the barn, Ghyllian and Tor had Finn's mane neatly braided, his hooves polished, and his coat glistening. "He's all ready," Ghyllian announced. "You two are going to look quite spiffy out there."

Samantha laughed and took Finn's lead. "We're going to have a good time, aren't we, fellow?" she asked the horse. Finn snorted and tossed his head.

"We'll see you in the arena," Tor said. "Good luck."

When it came their turn to test, Finn's movements were precise, his responses to Samantha's cues immediate, and he seemed to be enjoying himself as they went through the controlled test.

"Great job!" Tor said when she saw how well they had placed. "Tomorrow is cross-country, and you know he'll blow the competition away there. Imagine, Sammy, you might place first in the horse trials!"

The next morning Samantha walked the cross-country course with Tor, reviewing the jumps and the lay of the land.

"This is going to be tough," Samantha said, eyeing a series of log jumps that wound through a copse of trees. Another jump, built like a staircase, required the horse to bound up two levels before leaping a fence at the top.

"It's going to be a challenge," Tor agreed. "But you and Finn won't have any problem. He won't hesitate for a second at any of these jumps. You'll be great, Sammy. I'm sure of it."

Samantha watched the first five riders negotiate the course. Three of them beat the optimal time, but the fourth horse went down in the lake jump, water splashing everywhere as the unseated rider landed on his back in the pond.

She mounted Finn as the fifth rider started the course, and watched the tall, blond German man, riding a bay Hanoverian, fly through the quarry obstacle, leaping up out of the shallow pit and over a stout log.

"His time is really good," she murmured to Finn. No sooner had she spoken than the pair came up on the puzzle, a challenging series of angled jumps. The horse went at the closest fence as his rider tried to head him for the shorter route, and in confusion, the horse balked at the jump.

"Refusal," Samantha said, feeling sorry for the

rider. "No matter how good their time, that's going to knock their points down a bunch."

When Samantha's turn came, she rode Finn to the arena and waited for the officials to signal her to start. As soon as they were on the course, Finn broke into an eager gallop, leaping over a wide flower bed, then sailing easily over a tall, wide log jump before racing across the open field toward the quarry. They quickly cleared the first few of the thirty-two jumps that made up the course. Finn felt strong and surefooted, giving Samantha the confidence to ask him for more speed. "We can do this," she murmured to the horse.

Finn stretched out willingly, covering the ground with distance-eating strides, rising into the air to sail over a hay wagon, then turned sharply to take another fence. After another few strides, they were at a pair of pickups, parked with their tailgates touching, their beds filled with brush. Samantha took a deep breath, squeezing her legs against Finn's sides, but she didn't need to force the horse to go for the jump. Finn leaped the strange obstacle without hesitation, and Samantha steered him toward the lake. Finn splashed through the water unfazed, and Samantha exhaled as they cleared the jump that took them out of the water.

Don't get too arrogant, she reminded herself. There were four more jumps to go, and anything could happen. Still, Finn was running strongly, and Samantha couldn't suppress a surge of excitement. But as they came over a simple flat jump called the wine bar, she felt Finn's leg buckle on the landing. He tried to keep running, but Samantha pulled him up and leaped from his back, lifting his right front leg to keep the weight off it until the officials could get to them.

"Oh, Finn," she moaned as he struggled to pull his leg free. "Stand quietly, boy, please." In the background she could hear the voices of the spectators, starting as a shocked murmur and increasing in volume as the horse ambulance rolled onto the course.

Samantha fought back tears as the vet wrapped Finn's leg and led the limping horse into the van.

"IT APPEARS HE HAS A SLIGHT BOW TO HIS TENDON," THE event veterinarian informed them. Jimmy, Ghyllian, Samantha, and Tor stood by Finn's stall in the veterinarian barn. Tor had his arm around Samantha's shoulders. Jimmy looked at her and smiled weakly.

"It wasn't anything you did, Samantha," he reassured her.

"But there's more," the veterinarian said, holding up the X rays he had taken of Finn's leg. "It looks like he has the beginnings of pedal osteitis." He sighed. "I don't know that he'll ever jump again."

"Pedal osteitis," Tor said, eyeing Finn. "That's the

same disease Red Rum had, and he still raced and won."

The vet nodded. "Rummie was an exceptional steeplechaser," he said. "One in a million."

"And Finn has Red Rum's blood in his veins," Jimmy told the vet. "Thank you for the diagnosis. We'll take him home and figure out what it is we can do for him."

The four of them were quiet during the return trip to Celtic Meadows. Samantha was close to tears the entire time. She tried to do as Jimmy had said and not blame herself for Finn's injury, but she still felt responsible for the horse.

Near home, Jimmy slapped the steering wheel of the truck. "I've got it!" he exclaimed. "I know what to do." He looked over at Samantha and smiled. "We're going to cure Finn, and I know exactly how."

"We're going to start working him in the ocean, aren't we?" Tor said, grinning at Jimmy.

"That's right," the Irishman said. "Just like the trainer Ginger McCain did with his sire. It helped Rummie, and it'll help Finn. His career isn't over. It's just beginning."

"Gallop him in the ocean?" Samantha asked.

Tor nodded. "It toughened Red Rum's feet and made his legs strong. Jimmy's right—it's definitely worth a try."

For the next several days Samantha and Ghyllian took turns soaking Finn's injured leg, grooming the horse while they did so that he would stand quietly with his foot in the bucket of water.

When Dr. Ainsworth, Celtic Meadows' vet, came to take new X rays, he nodded in approval at what he saw.

"The tendon looks good," the vet said. "I do see some slight bone deterioration, and we can check him periodically, but right now there's little else we can do. If I were you, I'd retire him to stud and forget his racing career."

After the vet left, Samantha stood petting Finn, gazing into the horse's limpid eyes.

"I don't care if both the vets say you're done," she told Finn. "I'll do everything I can to help you get better. You love to race too much to give up now."

Tor nodded. "That's the spirit," he said, then glanced at his watch. "We have plenty of time today," he said. "Let's get started with the salt water therapy."

Samantha recognized the determined set to his

jaw, and she couldn't help smiling. She knew that Tor was as stubborn as she was, and once he set his mind to something, he'd make sure it happened.

"We'll get him sound again, Sammy," Tor said. "I know we can do it."

For several days Samantha walked Finn in the waves at the edge of the beach, leading him through the water, and at night she'd wrap his legs, feeling the length of his cannon bones, trying to tell if she could feel any difference.

"I don't know about Finn," Ghyllian commented one morning, "but I think your legs are getting stronger, too."

Samantha laughed. "I sure can feel my muscles when we come back from our walks on the beach," she admitted. "Maybe it's as good a treatment for getting riders in shape as it is for horses."

The next morning they trailered Finn and another of the Celtic Meadows horses, Slattery, to the beach. Finn tossed his head excitedly, inhaling the salty air, and pranced in place. "Do you think I should just lead him in the water again?" Samantha asked as Tor saddled Slattery.

Tor shook his head. "Tack him up," he said. "He's making excellent progress, Sammy. It's time to get back in the saddle for both of you." Samantha jogged Finn in the water that day and was pleased to feel the evenness of his gait and the power in his strides.

On some of their daily trips, Ghyllian accompanied them with Bridget, her bay mare, and the three of them worked their horses in the water.

"My dad says it toughens their tendons, and the salt water is good for their feet," she informed Samantha. "He agrees with Tor that Finn will come around."

After a solid month of working in the water, Finn seemed stronger than ever. Samantha was encouraged enough to let him gallop in the shallow waves, and she could tell by his action that he was ready to do more. When they returned to the farm that afternoon, Tor called the vet to have him check Finn over again.

"Of course he isn't cured," Dr. Ainsworth said after he had examined Finn. "But the condition of his bones is stable, and that's a very good thing." He stood back and folded his arms across his chest. "Whatever you're doing with this horse," he said, looking from

Tor to Samantha, "keep it up. He looks excellent."

"Then it's time to prep him for a steeplechase," Jimmy said, looking at Samantha.

"Do you really think that's a good idea?" Samantha asked, eyeing Finn uncertainly. "Maybe we'd better just let him take it easy."

Jimmy shook his head. "It won't make his condition any worse," he said, glancing at the vet.

"He's right," Dr. Ainsworth said, closing his bag. "Eventually Finn won't be able to run, of course, but while he can, I suggest you let him do what he was bred to do."

Samantha caught her lower lip in her teeth. "Do you really think he's ready?"

"Look at him," Dr. Ainsworth said to Samantha. "He's in top condition, as sound as he can be, and bred for the chase. I don't care much for steeplechases—I think they're hard on the horses. But if you're going to race him, now's the time."

"And you're in top condition yourself, Samantha," Jimmy said. "All those weeks of walking Finn in the water have put muscles on you, too. I think you're both ready for a steeplechase."

Samantha looked at Tor. "Then I guess it's time for you to start coaching both of us," she said.

* * *

"Let's take the horses out for a bit of cross-country,"
Tor told Samantha a couple of mornings later. They
were standing in the eventing horse barn at Celtic
Meadows, watching the horses enjoy the balmy
weather. "Jimmy is determined that you're going to
chase him at Punchestown next week."

Samantha wrinkled her nose. "I'm still not all that
sure about riding in an Irish steeplechase," she said.
"Why can't you race him?"

Tor lowered his brows, giving her a stern look.
"You know as well as I do that you're the best jockey
for him. I'd love to ride him, but we've all watched
him when you're in the saddle. I know he'll run his
heart out for you. I see it, Jimmy sees it—even Joe has
said he's never seen a horse try harder for anyone. If
Finn is going to make a good showing, he needs your
help to do it."

Samantha knew that what Tor had said was
true. When she worked Finn on the flat track, his
times were always better than when Tor rode him,
and the horse trusted her completely when it came
to negotiating the tall brush fences Tor had them
jumping.

"It sounds like I'm outnumbered," Samantha said.

"I wouldn't encourage you to chase here if I didn't have all the confidence in the world in your riding skills," Tor added.

Samantha exhaled and nodded. "I don't think I have much choice," she said. "I'll get Finn ready, if you want to tack Slattery up, and we can hit the trails."

While Tor saddled the big black gelding he rode regularly, Samantha tacked Finn, carefully wrapping his legs before she took the time to brush out his silky brown mane. "You do want to race, don't you," she said, running a soft rag along his glossy flank. Every time she saddled the horse to exercise him, Finn would get so wound up that she could hardly hold him back. That day was no different. He pranced excitedly as she saddled him, and Samantha patted his tense shoulder.

"I think I'm the only one *not* excited about racing at Punchestown," she told him. "It looks like I'm not going to get out of this one." Finn snorted, tossing his head as Samantha gathered the reins and swung onto the saddle.

In a short time Tor and Samantha were headed down the lane toward their favorite trails. Slattery pranced, expending his energy in a parked canter as they rode along the side of the road.

"Maybe I should have used him for my dressage test at Badminton," Samantha joked, admiring the gelding's arched neck and the set of his elegant head. The eight-year-old gelding loved to jump and would fly over anything Tor asked him to. With Slattery, Tor had developed a reputation as a solid competitor on the local racetracks, but the black didn't have Finn's breeding or his racing talent.

But whenever Tor raced, Samantha would stand at the side of the track, her heart in her throat during the entire race. Not only were the Irish courses more difficult than the ones they'd ridden in Kentucky, but the jockeys seemed more aggressive, the horses more fearless. She had seen Tor come off at some of the fences, and she'd held her breath until he scrambled to his feet and remounted his horse to rejoin the race.

Slattery tossed his head, trying to pick up the pace as they rode side by side along the path. "He's full of himself today," Tor commented, keeping the energetic horse in check.

Samantha was busy keeping Finn in line, but she darted a look at Tor's mount. The gelding pranced, tugging at the reins and challenging Tor every step of the way. Tor smiled, patting Slattery's neck. "I guess we need to find another chase for you to run in," he said, then glanced at Samantha. "When we take Finn to race in Kildare, maybe we'll take Slattery, too."

Samantha nodded, gazing at the low hills ahead of them. "That's a good idea," she said. "Then I wouldn't have time to worry about myself. I'd be too concerned for your safety."

"You'll be fine," Tor reassured her, sitting easily to Slattery's gait.

Finn tugged at his reins, picking up on the other horse's energy. "They're aching to stretch out a bit," Samantha said, keeping a tight rein on her mount. And she had to admit that she was looking forward to a good cross-country gallop herself. Although the crowded steeplechase races made her tense, she still loved the feeling of a fast-paced run, the challenge of taking the jumps and negotiating the unexpected turns and drops they came across. And she knew Finn felt the same way.

The trail they were on opened up, and they both spotted a low stone fence across a meadow of emerald grass. Tor and Samantha shared a look, and without a word, both leaned over their horses' shoulders and let the eager Thoroughbreds go.

The exhilarating gallop across the meadow sent the blood rushing through Samantha's veins. She darted a glance sideways and saw Tor and Slattery keeping pace with Finn and her. She pressed her fists into Finn's neck, urging him to speed up, watching closely as the fence loomed large in front of them.

She rose in the stirrups as Finn came off the ground, balancing herself as he jumped the wide wall, then settled back onto the saddle as they raced away from the jump.

"Great one!" Tor yelled, aiming Slattery toward another fence, pulling ahead of Samantha and Finn.

"Are we going to let them get the better of us?" Samantha asked her horse, crouching in the saddle as they galloped across the meadow. In the distance a brook meandered along the edge of the meadow, the sunlight sparkling on the water. The slight breeze felt warm on her face, and the sound of the horses' hooves thundering on the ground echoed in her ears. Samantha inhaled deeply, her senses sharpened with the adrenaline rush she felt. Even though she was a little intimidated by the idea of competing in an Irish steeplechase, she knew that when she was racing the way they were just then, she felt more alive than at any other time. She urged Finn to pick up his speed, and the horse lengthened his strides, galloping confidently toward the next jump.

In a moment they were over it, and Samantha tightened his left rein, heading them toward the wide brook.

"Water jump!" she called to Tor.

As they crossed the meadow, Finn's powerful strides pulled them ahead of Slattery, and Samantha grinned to herself. "That's my boy," she told the horse, who swiveled his ears back at the sound of her voice. "Let's show them how to jump that stream."

She eyed the distance, calculating the strides before they needed to take off to clear the water, and as Finn sailed into the air, she gripped his mane, enthralled with the sense of weightlessness that came with the jump.

Finn landed on the far side, but behind her Samantha heard a splash, and she glanced back to see Slattery scrambling out of the water, Tor clinging to his back, laughing.

Samantha turned Finn and cantered back to the brook.

"We came up a bit short," Tor explained as she stopped at his side.

"So I see," Samantha replied. "But it was a dandy race while it lasted."

"And you'll do as well at Punchestown," Tor said. "Just ride as though you're the only ones on the track, all right?"

"It's hard to forget there are fifteen other horses when they're shoulder to shoulder going over the jumps," Samantha replied as they walked the horses along the brook to cool them out.

"And Finn will be the greatest one there," Tor told her. "I know it."

"I'm still not so sure about this," Samantha told Tor, looking around at the back area of the Punchestown racetrack. "I really don't think I'm good enough, Tor."

"You'll be fine, Sammy." Tor put his hands on her shoulders and looked into her eyes, his expression serious. "Do you think Jimmy and I would encourage you to race if we didn't believe in you?"

Samantha heaved a deep sigh. "I know," she said. "But I still have butterflies stampeding in my stomach."

"And rightfully so," Jimmy said, coming around

the corner of the trailer. "That'll keep you on your toes." He patted Samantha's shoulder. "But I've watched you handle Finn in some pretty tense situations, and I know you two will be able to hold your own out there. Now you go change into my silks and get weighed in for the race. We'll see you on the track."

Samantha picked up her bag, and Tor gave her a quick kiss. "For luck," he said.

Samantha smiled nervously, then headed across the crowded grounds to the dressing rooms. She passed trainers and jockeys huddled together, talking about the upcoming races, and grooms leading powerful-looking jumpers toward the saddling area. Closer to the track, Samantha could see a large crowd of spectators gathering. The weather was perfect for a day at the races. The summer sun warmed the air, and the blue sky over Kildare stretched as far as Samantha could see.

It's going to be a good race, she told herself. *And if all goes well, it'll be the first of many.*

"Samantha, over here." Samantha stopped as Molly walked up to her. Her friend was wearing a jacket embroidered with the name of the farm she and Joe owned, Claddagh Stables. Molly had her hair tied back, and her freckled face was shining with excitement. "Joe's riding today, too," she told Samantha. "He's got a new horse to ride, and he's quite excited about taking this new one over the fences."

Samantha gnawed at her lower lip and nodded. "I wish I could say the same about my race."

"Ah, you'll be fine," Molly said. "You've walked this track so many times, you could ride it in your sleep."

"I'll be wide awake today, believe me," Samantha said. "The thing that still throws me off is riding in the opposite direction of what we do in the States."

"You adapted to driving on the left side of the road quickly," Molly reminded her. "This isn't any different from that."

When Samantha raised her eyebrows, Molly laughed. "Well, maybe a little different."

"When is Joe racing?" Samantha asked, looking around for Molly's husband.

"He's in the fourth race," Molly said, holding up a program. "Riding against Tor. Won't that be a grand race to watch? I'm glad he isn't riding against you. He'd be unbearable if an American beat him." She winked at Samantha. "Even if the American sounds like she's lived in County Kildare all her life."

Samantha laughed, the fluttering in her stomach subsiding as she relaxed a little. "It's pretty hard not to pick up that Irish brogue," she admitted, then glanced at her watch. "I'd best be getting over to the lockers," she told Molly. "I don't have a lot of time before the first race."

"I'll be cheering you on," Molly promised, waving good-bye to Samantha and turning to disappear into the throngs of people milling about the grandstand.

There were only a few female jockeys racing that day, and after Samantha had weighed in with the clerk of the scales, she had the small women's dressing room to herself. She quickly donned her breeches, then pulled the Celtic Meadows shirt over her head, looking down to admire the green shamrocks scattered over a white background. She tucked the shirt into the pants and pulled on her tall boots, then bound her long hair into a tight braid and gazed at her reflection in the mirror over the sink. "This is it, Samantha," she said aloud. "Your first Irish steeplechase, and you are going to rock."

She made her way to the parade ring, where Ghyllian was holding Finn, waiting for her. The girl gave her a nod. "You look fantastic in Celtic Meadows' colors," Ghyllian told her.

"Thanks," Samantha replied, looking around at the other jockeys. The rest of the riders were men, all taller than Samantha and very athletic-looking. "I don't know why your dad and Tor think I'm ready to compete against this bunch, though."

"Maybe on a flat track the fastest horse and the fittest rider have the best odds," Ghyllian reminded her. "But you know perfectly well that anything can happen in a steeplechase." She laughed. "I remember one upset where the slowest horse on the track won because of a pileup over one of the jumps. He was going at such an easy pace that he missed all the accidents and came in first."

Samantha grimaced. "I doubt Finn will be the slowest horse on the track today," she said. "I just hope we manage all those jumps and finish the race together."

"Up you go, then," Ghyllian said, nodding toward Finn. She gave Samantha a leg up, and they joined the other horses and jockeys so that the fans could preview the horses. People pressed against the parade-ring fence, looking over the horses, before they rushed off to place their last-minute bets.

Finally they were on the track, and Samantha kept circling Finn at the starting line, keeping the eager horse from a false start. She kept an eye on the starter, and when she saw the flash of red as the flag came down, she leaned over the stallion's shoulders and they plunged forward, shoulder to shoulder with the horses on both sides of them.

8

SAMANTHA KEPT HER EYES LOCKED ON THE JUMP IN FRONT of them, forcing herself to ignore the horses crowding Finn on both sides. Her ears were filled with the snorted breaths of the running horses, the voices of the other jockeys, and the distant roar of the crowd in the grandstand. Over it all, she could hear the voice of the announcer blaring from the loudspeakers.

"It's a great start for the first race, with number seven, Revenge, and number sixteen, White Cliff, taking an early lead, with the rest of the field on their heels!"

Finn cleared the first fence easily, keeping pace with the other horses. As the riders spread out on the track, Samantha could see several horses move ahead of them. Finn tugged at the reins, trying to get Samantha to give him his head, but she held him back. "We've got three miles and twenty-eight fences to clear, boy," she said, moving into jumping position as they flew over the next fence. "You don't want to run yourself out in the first half."

Under the tense excitement she felt, Samantha was still worried about Finn's leg. Even with Dr. Ainsworth's assurance that the tendon was fine, she couldn't help replaying the jump at Badminton, when she had felt him stumble, and as they landed after each jump she braced herself for that same awful feeling.

As they cleared the third fence, Samantha caught a glimpse of the horse to their right catching its front legs on the wall. The horse somersaulted, sending the rider tumbling onto the track.

"Number six is down!" the announcer cried. "Jockey Tom Short is out early in the race, but horse and rider appear fine, and they're clearing the track! We've still got twenty-nine riders going strong, with number seven, Revenge, in the lead, followed closely by Madcap and Intrepid!"

As Finn galloped toward the fourth jump Samantha glanced back and saw two other horses go down at the third fence.

"The third jump is taking a huge toll on the field today," the announcer called. "Three down, twenty-seven left in the field, with Revenge still holding the lead!"

We're still in the running, Samantha told herself, turning her attention to the next fence. It looked like a simple jump, but she knew there was a drop on the other side that caught many horses by surprise. There were at least a dozen horses ahead of them on the track, all of them running strong and jumping cleanly.

"We may not win this race, Finn," she told the horse, "but we'll do our best to finish it together, won't we?" Two more horses went down on the next fence, and Samantha steered Finn wide, barely missing one of the fallen horses as it scrambled to its feet.

"Now the water jump and the turn," she said aloud, letting Finn open up a bit as they headed for the tricky obstacle. Both Joe and Tor had given her specific instructions about the jump, and she ran their advice through her head. *Go for the inside. Then you'll have room to take the corner even if it takes you a second to regroup after you land.*

But as they approached the fence, she could see

several more horses going down as they tangled with each other, all of them crowded at the inside edge of the track.

"We've lost six more," the announcer cried. "They're dropping like flies today, and we have two runaways on the track. We're down to nineteen horses, and we're not even halfway through the first race. It's going to be a busy day for the medics if this keeps up!"

As he spoke, a riderless horse galloped past Samantha and Finn, its reins flapping, its head high. The horse swerved in front of them, and Samantha checked Finn, giving the out-of-control horse plenty of room.

"We're aren't going to save any track here," she muttered, angling Finn toward the outer side of the jump. The area was clear of horses, but they would have to cut it close to make the corner without brushing up against the outside rail.

"No different from some of those tricky jumps at Badminton, boy," she told him, knowing she was reassuring herself more than the horse. Finn galloped boldly at the fence and leaped into the air. Even as they jumped, Samantha swallowed a lump of fear, not for herself but for Finn. If he strained the tendon again because of her decisions during the race, she would never forgive herself.

But Finn landed cleanly on the far side, and Samantha let him take a single stride before turning him away from the rail. The inside of the track was clear of horses, and they cut across the turf toward the inside rail. If they wanted to have any chance of catching up with the lead horses, they needed to make up time, and that meant running on the inside.

The two riderless horses were still on the track, galloping ahead of them, zigzagging down the turf, jumping some fences and running around others, as people tried to catch them. *If this were a flat-track race at home,* Samantha thought, *they'd end the race right now.* A runaway horse was dangerous, and she'd seen some horrible wrecks because of loose horses on the racetrack. But she couldn't think about it. This was Ireland, and the racing rules were different.

As they started the second circuit of the race, Samantha was sure at least half the riders were gone. She darted a look behind her, surprised at the number of horses still in the race. She and Finn were neck and neck with five other horses, all of them running steadily, and there were two horses ahead by at least four lengths.

"You have lots left, don't you, boy?" Samantha asked, leaning over Finn's shoulders as she loosened her grip on his reins. In response, the well-conditioned horse shifted his speed up a gear. They pulled ahead of the bunch they were running with, and soon they were closing in on the two lead horses.

Finn seemed to be running easily. Even though his coat was dark with sweat, his breathing sounded good, and his long legs devoured the turf as they flew along the track. The fences seemed like blurs of green beneath them as Finn fought to catch up with the front-runners, and Samantha could hear the announcer yelling as they drew close to the lead horses.

"It's Finn McCoul making a move! Finn McCoul and Samantha Nelson are closing the gap! Number twenty-three is running like he has wings on his feet!"

As they came into the corner with the water jump for the second time, they were within half a length of the lead horses. Samantha took a deep breath, moving Finn to the inside, as Tor and Joe had said to do. "I hope those two clear the jump," she murmured, eyeing Revenge and Norseman, the two horses ahead of them. She tightened her hands on the reins as they followed the other horses over the fence, heaving a sigh of relief when they landed. Finn dashed after the first- and second-place steeplechasers.

"Clean jumps by Norseman, Revenge, and Finn McCoul," she heard the voice over the loudspeaker announce. "But it looks like Revenge is flagging, and Finn McCoul is moving up on him like a locomotive! The brown horse may have a chance of winning his very first chase!"

Ahead of her, Samantha could see that Revenge, who had held the lead from the start, was wearing down. His strides seemed labored, and Samantha felt pity for the horse. He had run a hard race, but it didn't look as though he was going to be able to keep up the hard pace for the last half mile.

"They're not going to get away from us, are they, Finn?" she asked, leaning over his shoulders and urging him to speed up. Finn responded immediately, stretching his legs, reaching his long neck out as they tore over the course, moving quickly into a three-way tie with the other two horses. Samantha knew the conditioning work they had done in the ocean had given Finn the stamina he needed to finish the race.

As they flew over the last jump, Revenge dropped

back, and Finn's flat-track breeding seemed to kick in. He dug in, stretching out farther than Samantha had imagined possible, pulling ahead of Norseman. The other jockey shot them a startled look and leaned over his mount's shoulders, bringing his whip down on his horse's hip. But Finn reached forward, his muscles bunching and straining.

"Come on!" Samantha cried as Norseman picked up speed, but Finn had another gear left, and it seemed to Samantha that the other horse had practically stopped running, he dropped back so quickly.

As they neared the finish line she glanced back to see Norseman several yards behind them and Revenge even further back, with the rest of the field still coming up on the last fence. Finn flew across the finish line alone, and Samantha could hear the crowd going wild. The announcer's excited voice filled the air.

"It was no contest for the American and her Irish horse! Samantha Nelson, the American jockey, brings Finn McCoul in for a win in the first race and sets a track record in her first win for Celtic Meadows!"

Tor, Ghyllian, and Jimmy dashed onto the track as she brought Finn to a stop and slid from the saddle.

"You won by five lengths!" Jimmy exclaimed,

pounding her on the back. "Five whole lengths!"

Samantha turned to Finn, who was sweat-soaked, white lather coating his shoulders, his chest heaving. "Finn did it, you mean," she said, feeling a little giddy about the win. "You're an awesome horse," she told him, running her hand along his jaw as Tor checked his legs.

"He looks fine," Tor announced, straightening up and patting Finn's shoulder. He grinned at Samantha. "You won your first steeplechase as though those other horses were standing still."

"He's obviously a cut above the other horses here," Jimmy said.

"Back in the saddle," Tor said, offering her a leg up. "It's time for glory in the winner's circle, and then off to cool this boy down."

As soon as she had weighed in and posed for photographs with Jimmy and Ghyllian standing by Finn's head, Samantha slipped her saddle from the horse's back and stepped aside so that Ghyllian could throw a cooling sheet over him.

"It's time we let him do what he was born to do, and start gearing up for the Grand National," Jimmy said. He looked at Samantha with a broad grin. "And of course you'll need to go into more intense training, too, so that the two of you will win the trophy for Celtic Meadows."

"Let us recover from this chase first!" Samantha exclaimed, laughing. But after the thrill of winning, and feeling just how strong Finn was, she knew she wanted to chase Finn in the Grand National, probably even more than Jimmy wanted her to.

"You're a tough coach," Samantha said to Tor one morning. She was lying on the living room floor doing sit-ups while Tor stood over her with his arms folded, counting the repetitions.

"You'll thank me when you and Finn are racing in the Grand National," he said with a grin. "And when we're done here, we need to get out to the barn so you can work Finn, too."

"It should be you riding him," Samantha replied, pulling herself up by her stomach muscles. She flopped back with a groan.

"You just want to be the one telling me how hard I need to work out," Tor said. "Now quit trying to distract me from counting and do ten more."

Samantha wrinkled her nose at him, then did as Tor had said, forcing herself to finish her tough exercise regimen. Tor was right. If she and Finn were going to compete against the top steeplechase horses and jockeys, they both needed to be in perfect condition.

"Listen to this," Jimmy said. Samantha and Tor were grooming Finn and Slattery after a strenuous morning work on the beach. In the months since their first win at Punchestown, Samantha and Finn had competed in several chases, and Finn had been a consistent winner, bringing a lot of media attention to the farm, himself, and his American jockey.

Samantha rested the brush against Finn's flank and glanced at the horse's owner. "I'm all ears," she said.

Jimmy held up the sports page of the paper and grinned. "It really isn't much different from the last several articles," he said. "But I still like to read them out loud." He gave a dramatic pause. "The headline says, 'Finn to Win.' How do you like that?" He didn't wait for Samantha or Tor to respond. "Then it says, 'Celtic Meadow's steeplechase wonder, Finn McCoul, the unstoppable son of Red Rum, has set the steeplechase world on its ear. Finn has rocked his way to the top of the class, proving himself to be a strong contender for glory at the Grand National.

121

Will Finn follow in his sire's hoofprints and win the race more than once? Finn and his jockey, Samantha Nelson, are the team to watch at Aintree for the upcoming race.'"

"Can you believe it?" Samantha asked, patting Finn's neck.

"I do," Tor said. "He's brilliant on the track." He smiled at Samantha. "And his jockey is pretty impressive, too."

Samantha looked from Tor to Jimmy. "I never thought I'd feel this way, but I'm really looking forward to the race."

"That's good," Jimmy said, holding up an envelope bulging with papers. "Because I went ahead and paid the fees. You and Finn are the twelfth entry in the Grand National." Jimmy grinned at Samantha. "You two are going to put Celtic Meadows' name on the front page of every paper. My American jockey is going to make the farm famous."

Samantha eyed Jimmy and shook her head. "But you're not putting any pressure on me, are you?"

Jimmy laughed. "Not a bit of it, Sammy," he said. "I'm just confident that you and Finn will sweep the field. I'm looking forward to our moment in the winner's circle, that's all."

Samantha smiled at Jimmy as she stroked Finn's glossy shoulder. "Finn and I are going to do our best to show everyone what a son of Red Rum can do, and give you your steeplechase champion."

For the next several weeks Samantha worked daily with Finn, with Jimmy, Tor, and sometimes Joe Flynn coaching her. One evening Joe and Molly came to the cottage for dinner, and Joe held out a videotape.

"We're going to review the Aintree course," he announced. "I don't have a horse for the race this year, and since I'm not going to be competing against you, Samantha, I'll do everything I can to give you and Finn an edge on the course."

They settled in the tiny living room, and Joe started the tape. "See," he said, pointing at the screen, "the opening straight isn't quite as easy as it looks. You have almost half an hour of tension mounting before the start, with the parade, checking your girth, and forty riders jockeying for the best view of the first jump. Don't make the mistake of trying to get into the lead early. Finn has the stamina and speed to fight his way through the no-hope horses and settle into a good position."

123

Tor nodded. "With four and a half miles to run, you'll have time to negotiate a good position."

Samantha eyed the horses taking the first jump, cringing as three horses went down immediately.

"It's the speed that gets them," Joe said. "Take the time to jump it right. If you can get past those first two, you can relax a little. Just remember, timing is everything."

After Joe and Molly left that evening, Samantha's mind was reeling with the information Joe had given her. She sent Tor to the barn while she washed the dinner dishes, trying to review everything she'd been told. *One week to go*, she said to herself, a tense shudder running through her as she recalled the video, replaying the falls at each of the fences, trying to keep track of the mistakes the jockeys had made.

When the phone rang, Samantha set the dinner plate she was washing back into the sink full of soapy water and dried her hands on her jeans before she picked it up. "Hello?" she said.

"Sammy?" Ian's voice sounded strange. "Is that you?"

"Of course it's me," she said. "Who else would be answering my phone, Dad?"

Ian chuckled, but the sound lacked mirth. "You just sound so . . . Irish."

"I do?" she said. "But we've only been here six years. I'm hardly Irish yet."

"I hear them talking about you on the news," Ian said. "They still call you the American jockey, so I guess you can't be too Irish. You just sound that way. How are things going there? Are you and Finn ready for the Grand National?"

"Oh, yes," Samantha said, smiling as she thought of the horse. "He's such an amazing animal, Dad. I can't imagine not being able to ride him. I only wish you and Beth could be here to watch us race."

"That isn't likely to happen," Ian said. "There's a lot going on here."

"Like what?" Samantha asked, concerned at how down her father sounded. "Is something going on that we need to know about?"

There was a pause before Ian spoke again. "That's why I called," he finally said. "Tor's father is in the hospital, and he isn't doing too well. Tor needs to come to Kentucky as soon as he can get a flight."

9

"I'm going to Kentucky with you," Samantha said stubbornly, folding her arms across her chest. "Your dad is my family, too, and if there's a crisis, we need to be there together." They were standing in the barn, outside Finn's stall, where Samantha had found Tor feeding the big stallion a carrot.

Tor frowned at her and shook his head. "You made a commitment to Jimmy, and that means you can't leave right now. You need to stay here at least until next week for the Grand National. It wouldn't be fair to Jimmy, Finn, or you for you to leave with me. You can fly home after the race if I'm not back by then."

Samantha shook her head. "No way, Tor," she said. "We're going together, and that's that."

Tor patted Finn's shoulder while he gazed at Samantha. "You've spent years working toward this race, Samantha. Besides, you know my dad would be really upset if you gave it up on his account. You need to stay here and race Finn."

"What's this I hear? Are you having second thoughts about the race, Sammy?"

They both turned at the sound of Jimmy's voice.

"We have a family problem," Samantha said.

"You two aren't having an argument, are you?" Jimmy asked. "I can't have my two favorite employees fighting with each other."

"It's Tor's dad," Samantha said quickly, filling Jimmy in on the phone call from Kentucky. "So you see, we have to go home, at least for a while."

Jimmy's brow creased with deep wrinkles as he frowned thoughtfully. "It would break my heart not to see you race Finn at Aintree," he said, eyeing Samantha. "But it would hurt me more if you put the race ahead of family." He looked at Finn, then at Samantha again. "I can ask Joe Flynn to ride Finn for us, and next year you'll be the jockey to take him to his second win. After all," he said with a grin, "he *is* Red Rum's son, and he's going to do just like his sire, right?"

Samantha nodded, the heaviness on her heart

lightening at Jimmy's encouraging words. "Maybe he'll do better than Rummie," she said. "Maybe Finn can win the race three years in a row."

"We'll just keep a positive attitude," Jimmy said, then turned to Tor. "You'd best call the airline and get your flight booked," he told him. "And don't forget to order tickets for two."

"He doesn't have to," Samantha said, offering Jimmy an apologetic smile. "I already took care of that. Our flight leaves tomorrow morning. All we need to do is pack a few things."

"Just a few things," Jimmy repeated. "Because you'll both be back before you know it."

Tor and Samantha went to bed early, but Samantha lay awake all night, thinking about giving up her chance to race in the greatest steeplechase ever, and worrying about Tor's father. Mr. Nelson had welcomed her into his home and had always treated her like his own daughter. Jimmy was right. There would be more chances to chase on Finn, but if Mr. Nelson's health was failing, she needed to be there for him as much as Tor did.

Jimmy drove them to the airport. He gave Samantha a long, fatherly hug, then turned to Tor, offering him a firm handshake, then pulling him into a quick embrace. "You're like a son to me," he said. "You've both been the best thing to happen at Celtic Meadows since Ghyllian was born, and I'll miss you both terribly." He brushed at his eye, and Samantha was sure she saw the glint of a tear on his cheek before he swept it away.

"Now get on that plane," Jimmy said, tilting his head toward the gate, where passengers were lining up for the flight. "Have a safe trip, and we'll see you again before you know it."

He turned and hurried away, leaving Samantha and Tor to join the other travelers. As they boarded their flight Samantha hesitated for a moment, looking behind her at the concourse. She felt a wrenching pull in her heart and wondered if she would ever see Ireland again. *It's only a visit home,* she reminded herself. But she had a feeling they were leaving their wonderful life behind for good.

Exhausted from the sleepless night, Samantha ate only a little of the meal the flight attendant served, then dozed off as the in-flight movie started, waking several hours later as the plane crossed the Atlantic Ocean, the sky changing colors as they went through time zones, night and day trading places as they traveled west. She turned to Tor, who was thumbing through a book he had grabbed at a stand in the airport.

"Do you think we'll be in Kentucky long?" she asked.

Tor sighed. "I don't know, Sammy," he said. "We'll stay as long as we need to, I guess."

Samantha nodded. "As long as your dad needs us," she said, then pulled a blanket over her shoulder and slept again until they arrived in New York to change flights for the trip to Kentucky.

Ashleigh was waiting at the Keeneland airport for them. "You two haven't changed a bit," Ashleigh said, throwing her arms around Samantha. "It's so good to see you both. I just wish you'd come back for a happier reason."

"It's good to see you, too," Samantha said, returning Ashleigh's embrace.

"Let's grab your bags and get going," Ashleigh said, turning to Tor. "I'm sure you want to see your father."

"How long has he been ill?" Tor asked as they hurried to the luggage pickup.

Ashleigh stared at the suitcases moving past them on the carousel. "Quite a while," she finally said, "but he didn't want anyone to tell you."

"Why not?" Samantha demanded, horrified at the thought that Tor's father's condition had been kept a secret from them.

"Because he said you were doing so well in Ireland, and he didn't want to disrupt your lives."

"That sounds like Dad," Tor said, shaking his head as he pulled their suitcases from the belt. They left the airport for the parking area, where Ashleigh had left her car.

"Do you want to go home first?" she asked as she climbed behind the wheel.

"We both slept on the plane," Samantha said, glancing at Tor. "We can go straight to the hospital."

Ashleigh was quiet as she drove toward Lexington, and Samantha stared out the window, watching the scenery flow past them, Tor's hand tightly gripped in hers. Her thoughts on Mr. Nelson, Samantha barely noticed the rolling pastures of bluegrass, the fine-boned Thoroughbreds in the fields, and the stately mansions they passed.

Ashleigh dropped them at the hospital entrance and drove away to find a parking spot, while Samantha and Tor hurried through the glass doors to the brightly lit reception area.

"Mr. Nelson," the woman at the desk repeated,

looking through her files to find his room number. "He's on the third floor, in room seventeen."

Samantha glanced at Tor. "That's the intensive care ward," she said, her heart sinking.

The receptionist directed them to the elevators, and in a minute they were outside room seventeen. Tor stopped to take a deep breath before he went inside. "I don't know what to expect," he told Samantha. "I'm almost afraid to see him."

Samantha caught his hand and gave it a squeeze. "We'll see him together," she said. "I'll be right with you, Tor."

He offered her a weak smile. "Thanks, Sammy. I really am glad you're here."

A pretty, middle-aged nurse was coming down the hall, carrying a tray, and she stopped in front of the doorway and smiled warmly at them. "You must be Samantha and Tor," she said. "Your father talks about both of you nonstop."

Samantha stared at the nurse, surprised that she would know who they were.

"I'm Helen," she said. "I've been taking care of your father while he's been here, and I've heard so much about the two of you, I feel like I know you both. He's shown me dozens of photos of you," she added, "and we watched the Badminton Horse Trials on television together, so I got to see you ride, Samantha."

She turned to Tor and held out the tray. "He'll be so shocked to see you," she said. "But I'm sure it will do him a world of good."

Tor accepted the tray but gave Helen a questioning look.

She smiled in understanding. "It's cancer," she explained. "I asked Ian to call you because I thought it might help your father with his recovery. He didn't want to have you both leave Ireland, but it seemed important."

Tor smiled at her. "Thank you," he said. "I'd never forgive myself if something happened and I was three thousand miles away."

Helen nodded. "I know," she said, then tilted her head toward the room. "Now get in there and see him," she urged.

Mr. Nelson was propped up in the bed, and when he saw Tor and Samantha come into the room, his eyes widened in disbelief. "You're here," he said, sounding shocked.

Samantha gazed at her father-in-law. He looked thin and pale, but his eyes were clear, and a broad smile stretched across his face.

"You should have called us," she scolded him.

"Where do you think Tor got that stubborn streak of his?" Mr. Nelson asked. "Now come closer so I can give you both a hug."

When he held his arms out, Tor went to the side of the bed and leaned over, giving his father a kiss on the cheek. "If you'd wanted us to visit, all you had to do was ask," he said teasingly. "You scared the daylights out of us, Dad. But now that we're here, we can take care of Whisperwood until you're back on your feet."

Mr. Nelson frowned a little, then looked from Samantha to Tor. "I think we need to have a family meeting," he said, then looked to the doorway, where Helen was waiting. He gestured to her, and the nurse came into the room and stood by the side of the bed. Mr. Nelson reached out and took her hand, then looked back at Tor and Samantha.

"First you need to know that Helen and I plan to get married." He smiled up at the nurse. "I'm so grateful that she came into my life."

Samantha clapped her hands together. "Married!" she exclaimed in delight. "That's wonderful!"

A smile crept across Tor's face. "I'm really happy for both of you," he said.

"There's something else we need to talk about," Tor's father continued. "With my health, Helen and I have agreed that I need to spend time in a warm, dry climate, so we're going to leave Kentucky and move to Arizona."

Samantha felt the shock of his words vibrate through her, and she looked at Tor, seeing a stunned expression on his face.

"You're going to give up Whisperwood?" Tor asked. "You've put your life into the place."

"And it's time for me to pass it on," Mr. Nelson said slowly. "I wasn't thinking about giving it up. I'd rather give it to you two."

Tor stared at his father. "Give us the farm?"

"I know that with the experience you've gained in Ireland, you could turn Whisperwood into a world-class eventing farm," Mr. Nelson said. Then his cheerful expression faded, and he looked at Samantha. "But I'm not trying to force you to move back here," he said. "Whisperwood is yours if you want it, but I'll support whatever you decide to do. You both know that, don't you?"

Samantha nodded silently, all the while feeling as if a door had shut behind her. If they had the chance to run Whisperwood, they needed to accept the offer. Which meant never returning to Ireland—and never seeing Finn again.

She felt Tor looking at her, and she gazed up at

135

him and nodded slowly, conveying her approval of whatever decision he made, without saying a word.

Tor looked back at his father. "We'll make you proud," he said. "We'll take good care of the farm, Dad."

Mr. Nelson smiled. "You've both already made me proud," he replied.

"It feels odd to be back here," Samantha said, standing in the middle of Whisperwood's yard, her hands on her hips.

Tor looked around at the barns and paddocks and nodded. "We don't have to do this," he said. "We can let Dad sell the place, and go back to Ireland."

Samantha shook her head. "No," she said. "It was a good time for us, but it's over now, and we're back home."

At the sound of hoofbeats on the drive, Samantha turned to see Christina Reese riding her big gray mare, Sterling Dream, toward them. Twelve-year-old Christina waved excitedly, urging Sterling into a brisk trot.

"Welcome home!" she exclaimed, stopping her mare in front of them and hopping from her back. "Mom said you guys are going to open an event training facility now that you're both experts! Can I sign up for lessons right now?"

Samantha laughed and patted Sterling's nose, then looked at Tor. "I think we have our first client," she said.

Tor looked at Sterling, then at Christina. "We won't take it easy on you," he warned her.

Christina gazed back evenly. "I don't expect you to," she said. "I want to be a world-class three-day-event rider, just like Sammy."

"Then it sounds like we have an opening for you," Tor said, nodding in approval. He glanced at his watch. "It's almost time for the race," he said, glancing from Samantha to Christina. "Would you like to put your horse up and watch the Grand National with us?"

"Sure!" Christina led Sterling to the barn while Samantha went into the house to turn on the television. In a few minutes Christina joined them, and the three settled onto the sofa to watch the prerace parade.

"There he is," Samantha said, pointing at the screen. "There's Finn McCoul."

"He's awesome," Christina said, leaning forward to watch the big brown stallion prance past the cameras.

"Yes, he is," Samantha agreed, eyeing Finn closely. "He's going to be great today."

When the race started, Samantha held her breath, watching Joe negotiate the crowded field, holding Finn back a little so that they didn't rush the first two fences. Three of the lead horses, speeding into the jumps, fell at the first fence, and she felt her heart in her throat as Joe took Finn to the outside edge of the third jump, a six-foot open ditch followed by a five-foot-high fence. The crowd of horses in the middle of the fence caused several more falls, but Finn made a clean jump and galloped on.

When they reached Becher's Brook, with its two-foot drop on the landing side, Samantha came off the sofa, her fisted hands pressed together. "Careful, Finn," she murmured as Joe moved the horse toward the inside of the track. As they sailed over the high wall Samantha felt the jump as though she were on the horse herself. They landed well, and Finn went into the turn still running strongly. Behind them, some of the horses and riders, surprised by the drop, tumbled, taking more of the competition out of the race.

"Careful at the Canal Turn, Joe," she said, as if the jockey could hear her. The sharp corner, with the wide canal on the landing side of the jump, ended the race for many of the horses. Samantha choked as Joe took Finn over the fence at an angle to reduce the turn when they landed. As they cleared the challenging jump a riderless horse crowded close to them, and Samantha nearly screamed as the runaway brushed up against Finn. Samantha sank back on the sofa as the other horse veered off, and Joe headed Finn for the next two jumps.

"There are at least ten horses down," Tor commented. "And they're coming up on the fifteenth fence."

"Finn can handle the Chair," Samantha said. "As long as he's got room, he'll be fine." But the course narrowed, crowding the field, and Samantha stared wide-eyed as Finn took the ditch and fence flanked on either side by other horses. As they cleared the sixteenth jump, a low water obstacle, Samantha exhaled heavily.

"Halfway through," she noted. As the horses started the second circuit of the grueling course, Finn looked strong, but Samantha knew she wouldn't be able to breathe easily until the race was over. Only eighteen horses were left, making the second round easier to negotiate, but she knew that anything could happen, and she kept her hands tightly clenched, urging Finn over the course as if the connection she had with the horse could reach across the miles between them.

"He's going to make it!" Christina exclaimed, clasping her hands together as Finn approached the last jump before the long straight stretch across the finish line.

But as Finn flew over the last fence of the race, Samantha saw him stumble, and she gasped in horror as the horse settled into a limping run, still trying to finish the race even as Joe attempted to stop him.

"No!" she cried, feeling tears well up in her eyes as the jockey brought the horse to a standstill, letting the other racers fly past them. "He's broken down!"

As the race ended, the cameras followed the winning horse, leaving Samantha sick with worry about Finn.

After Christina had left Whisperwood, Samantha called Celtic Meadows, trying to get word on Finn's condition, but no one at the barn had any information for her.

"I'll have Jimmy call you as soon as he can," John, the head groom, promised.

Samantha hung up the phone, dejected.

"I'm sorry, Sammy," Tor said, wrapping his arms around her. "I wish you'd stayed and raced him. Maybe that wouldn't have happened."

Samantha leaned back and looked up at her husband, then shook her head. "Whatever happened with Finn might have happened if it had been me on him, too," she said. But she felt sick about the horse, not knowing his condition. "I'm going out to the barn to take care of the horses here," she told Tor. "I need to keep busy until we get word from Jimmy."

Several hours later when the phone rang, she let Tor get it, and waited tensely for him to pass on the message. Eventually he came over to where she was mucking out a stall, jabbing her pitchfork into the soiled bedding with rigid motions, prepared to hear the worst.

"It's a torn tendon," he told her, leaning his arms on the top of the stall wall. "At this point it doesn't look as though Finn will ever be able to race again."

Samantha stopped shoveling and looked up at him. "So what is Jimmy going to do with Finn?" she asked.

Tor shook his head. "He hasn't decided yet," he replied. "I'm sorry, Sammy. I guess we should have stayed in Ireland."

Samantha looked at Tor's face. She knew that Tor had enjoyed their life there as much as she had, but then she thought of Mr. Nelson and the joy in his face when they had agreed to take over Whisperwood. Their years of working for Jimmy, of racing and training in Ireland, had given them the knowledge and experience they needed to run a great eventing facility, and with Mr. Nelson's generosity, they had been given the chance to do just that.

She forced herself to smile and reached out to pat Tor's hand. "No," she said. "We did the right thing by coming home." But deep inside she wondered if they had made the right choice in coming back to Kentucky. Tor kept telling her she had the luck of the Irish, but maybe it wasn't her Irish luck but Ireland that had made them lucky.

10

Samantha finished feeding the mares, pausing to pet Miss Battleship before she pushed the wheelbarrow past the empty stall that had once been Shining's. With only Top Hat, Sierra, and Miss Battleship at Whisperwood, the first thing Samantha and Tor had done was to open the facility up to students who wanted to board their horses at the farm.

"Just until we get things going here," Tor had assured Samantha. "At some point we'll have our own horses in training, and that will keep us plenty busy, but for now we need the income that boarding brings in."

Samantha agreed, but she wondered if they would

ever find the right foundation stallion to start breeding their own eventing horses.

It will all work out, she thought. *We can do just as well in Kentucky as we could in Ireland. We had a lot of great years there, and now we own our own farm.*

But Finn was constantly in her thoughts. She had called Celtic Meadows several times in the last couple of weeks to check on the horse, but no one had answered the phone, and she was afraid something bad had happened to the stallion.

"You look like you could use a little fun," Tor said, coming out of the barn office. "How about taking a little drive with me?"

Samantha stared at him. "Where to?"

"It'll be a surprise," Tor replied, smiling. "Trust me, I think it will do you a world of good."

"I'm fine, really," Samantha said, reaching up to pat his cheek. "It's just taking longer than I expected to adjust to being back here."

"I'm afraid you're having second thoughts," Tor said, gazing down at her. "You've been awfully quiet in the month that we've been here."

Samantha shook her head. "I'm worried about Finn," she admitted. "It isn't being back in Kentucky that bothers me. But I've tried to call Celtic Meadows

144

to check on his progress several times in the last week, and no one ever returns my calls."

Tor shrugged. "I expect Jimmy's busy with the new eventing stable managers," he said. "I'm sure Finn is just fine. The last time I talked to Jimmy, Finn's bowed tendon was healing pretty well. And just because he won't be able to jump anymore doesn't mean he can't start siring offspring that could jump the moon."

"You're right," Samantha said. "And I guess taking a drive wouldn't hurt. Let me finish putting things away here, and we can go."

When they left the farm in Tor's pickup, she gazed out the window, enjoying the scenery. "Kentucky is a beautiful place," she said, looking out at the white-fenced pastures and the graceful horses that grazed in the meadows along the road. But when Tor took the turn that led to the Keeneland racetrack, she frowned at him. "You're taking me to the track?" she asked. "There aren't even any races going on today, and it's too late for the Keeneland auction."

Tor ignored her, and when they wound up not at the track but at the airport, Samantha gave him another piercing look. "Are we picking someone up?" she asked, but Tor just shook his head. When he pulled into the long-term parking area, she folded her arms in front of her. "I'm not leaving the car until you tell me what you're up to," she told him.

Tor made a face at her. "Don't spoil my surprise," he said. "Just cooperate, okay, Sammy?"

With a reluctant sigh she followed him into the airport. "If we're not meeting anyone, then we must be going somewhere," she said.

"That's right," Tor replied, leading her to the ticket counter. He produced a pair of airline tickets, but Samantha didn't ask any more questions, knowing her husband wasn't going to give her any straight answers. She followed him to the gates, and when the call came for a flight to New York, he took her hand and they got in line to board the plane.

"What in heaven's name are we going to New York for?" she demanded as they settled onto their seats.

"You'll see," Tor said mysteriously. "Just sit back and enjoy the trip, okay?"

"You are driving me crazy," Samantha said with a groan, but she found herself enjoying the adventure, knowing that whatever Tor had in mind, he wanted her to have a good time.

When they landed at Stewart International Airport in Newburgh, New York, Samantha walked off the plane, looking around curiously. "Why here?" she asked.

"The truth is," Tor replied, "there's a horse here I want to check out. Now that we've got Whisperwood, it's time we found the right foundation stallion to start breeding our eventing horses, and I think I might have located the right one."

"Oh," Samantha said, her sense of adventure fading. While she knew it wasn't fair to compare other horses to Finn, she was certain she'd never find another one like him, and she thought it would be discouraging even to look at other horses.

"This way," Tor said, guiding her through the busy airport. They caught a trolley and soon were approaching a large fenced compound full of big buildings.

"'United States Department of Agriculture New York Animal Import Center,'" she read aloud from the sign on the fence.

The guard at the gate greeted them with a friendly smile, and Tor pulled a packet of papers from his jacket, handing them to the man. After a quick inspection, the guard let them in, pointing toward one of the larger buildings in the compound. "Your animal is housed in that barn," he said.

Her curiosity getting the better of her, Samantha followed Tor to the building, where a woman in a white lab coat stopped them, checked their identification, and smiled.

"He's in stall number seven," she said. "You can go visit him now." She led them down the aisle of enclosed stalls. Samantha could hear horses behind the solid walls, some shuffling in their bedding, others whinnying and nickering to each other.

"Where did this horse come from?" she asked as they neared the stall. "How did you find out about him?"

"Oh," Tor said, "you'll see. This is the most special horse on the planet, I guarantee you."

"I left the most special horse on the planet in Ireland," Samantha said sadly.

As soon as she spoke, she heard a familiar nicker, and her heart skipped a beat. "Finn," she gasped, her heart speeding up as a soft whinny followed the nicker. "Finn is here!"

The attendant opened the wooden door, and Finn McCoul pressed his nose through the gap, inhaling a snorted breath as he took in Samantha's scent.

"Finn!" she cried, squeezing into the stall.

The big stallion grunted softly, rubbing his nose against the front of her shirt, and Samantha felt tears

148

start to stream down her cheeks. She turned to Tor, who stood in the doorway.

"How did you do this?" she asked, running her hands down the sides of the horse's sleek brown neck. "How did you get him here?"

Tor smiled. "Jimmy and I worked out a deal," he said. "I would have talked it over with you first, but more than anything, I wanted to give you the best surprise I could think of."

"Oh, my gosh, Tor, you have," Samantha said breathlessly, wrapping her arms around Finn's muscular neck. "Is he really here to stay? He's ours to keep?"

Tor nodded. "Finn is part of Whisperwood now, Sammy," he said. "Jimmy wanted you to have your own wee bit of Ireland, as he put it, and he thought Finn was the right part of Ireland for you to have. Of course, he'll be in quarantine here for a while, but then we'll have him shipped to Whisperwood to stand at stud as our foundation stallion for breeding our own jumpers. As soon as we get home, we can start fixing up the right stall for your new horse."

Samantha released a shaky sigh and turned from the horse to wrap her arms around Tor's neck. "Thank you," she murmured.

"I really didn't do anything," Tor protested. "If it

hadn't been for our families, we never would have met Finn in the first place, and if Jimmy hadn't hired us, we never would have spent the years we did in Ireland. Thanks to that experience, we're more than ready to run our own farm, and now we're able to have the best stallion we can to start our breeding program."

"I am so lucky," Samantha said with a happy sigh, pressing her face into Tor's neck. "I married the perfect man, and it doesn't matter where we are—we're going to have a wonderful life together."

Tor nodded, reaching past Samantha to stroke Finn's sleek nose. "Yes, we are," he agreed. "And thanks to you, wherever we are, we'll always have lots of good Irish luck."

11

"WOW," KAITLIN SAID, LEANING AGAINST THE STALL WALL behind her. "What a great story. Tor's dad is okay now, isn't he?"

"Oh, yes," Samantha said. "He and Helen are living in Arizona. They're both really happy there. They usually come out to visit for a few weeks in the summer, but they both like the desert." She reached up and petted Finn again. "Jimmy and Hannah retired, and Ghyllian sold off most of their jumpers. Celtic Meadows is a full-time flat-track facility now. They even had a horse run in the Preakness last year."

"Do you still see them?"

Samantha shook her head. "I missed seeing Ghyllian when she was in New York, but we keep in touch as much as we can."

"Hey, Sammy!" Cindy came down the barn aisle, a grin on her paint-spattered face. "It's time to check out the nursery."

Samantha and Kaitlin stood up as Cindy neared Finn's stall. "You're done already?" Samantha asked.

Cindy cocked her head and smiled at her sister. "It's been hours since we started," she said. "In fact, Ashleigh and Christina just got back from town. They picked up a pizza so that we can celebrate finishing the job."

"I need to get home," Kaitlin said, looking at her watch. "I didn't realize how long I'd been here."

"I spent a lot of time bending your ear," Samantha said apologetically. "I didn't mean to keep you so long."

"I'm glad you did," Kaitlin said. "Thanks for telling me about Finn." She petted the stallion before leaving the barn, and Cindy and Samantha headed for the house.

The enticing smell of fresh pizza wafted from the kitchen, and Samantha pressed her hand to her stomach. "I'm starving," she announced. "I think I could eat a whole pizza by myself. I hope you brought plenty."

Ashleigh laughed and nodded. "We picked up

two," she told Samantha. "I didn't even bother changing into clean clothes before I went." With a wave of her hand she indicated her paint-smeared jeans and shirt. "I was too hungry to care what people thought of me."

Samantha glanced at the dining table, set with plates, glasses of milk, and the boxes of warm pizza.

"Before we eat, I have to see the room," she said. Ashleigh and Cindy hurried down the hallway, disappearing into the bedroom.

Tor stood at the end of the hall, a broad grin on his face. "Wait until you see what they did," he told Samantha, taking her hand and leading her down the hall. "Now close your eyes," he ordered her.

Samantha complied, letting Tor position her in front of the open door. "Okay," Cindy said. "You can look now."

Samantha opened her eyes to see bright paint on the walls, which had been decorated with cartoon characters, and a cheerful mobile hanging from the ceiling. She gaped at an oak rocking chair, matching changing table, dresser, and crib, then pressed her hands to her mouth, her eyes wide as she took in the completed room. "Where did you get this furniture?" she asked, amazed at the room's transformation.

"It was a gift from Ben," Cindy said. "He wanted to do something special for the baby."

Ashleigh and Christina stood in the middle of the room, grinning at Samantha. Christina's face was speckled with paint. "Can you tell I did the ceiling?" she asked.

"You look wonderful," Samantha said, crossing the room to give Christina's shoulder a squeeze. "In fact, you three are the most beautiful people in the world to me."

"You guys did a fantastic job," Tor said.

Samantha spun slowly around to take in the room again, shaking her head in disbelief. "But I still can't get over the furniture."

She gave Tor a look, and he shrugged. "I didn't know anything about it," he said. "The delivery truck showed up, and they started unloading all this."

"Completely amazing," Samantha said, overwhelmed by the generosity of her friends.

"I'm going to wash up so we can have pizza," Christina told Samantha. She, Ashleigh, and Cindy left the room, leaving Tor and Samantha to admire the finished work. Samantha stood in the newly decorated nursery, her arm around Tor's waist, imagining what it would be like in another four months, when it was in use.

"I think it's time you told them," Tor reminded her, and Samantha nodded.

"I will," she said.

When they sat down to eat, Samantha tapped the side of her glass with a fork. "We have an announcement to make," she said, looking around the table.

"We already know," Cindy said, rolling her eyes. "You're expecting a baby."

"Thanks for stating the obvious," Samantha said with a laugh. "That isn't what I need to tell you."

"Then what?" Ashleigh asked, setting a slice of pizza on her plate.

"There's a little problem with the room," Samantha said, forcing a glum expression on her face.

"What?" Christina exclaimed, setting down the piece of pizza she was holding to stare at Samantha.

"No way," Cindy said. "We used all the right paint, didn't we? You don't like the color? What do you want changed?"

"It isn't that," Samantha said, dropping her gaze to her plate so that her friends couldn't see the grin lurking on her face.

"Then what is it?" Ashleigh demanded, leaning forward and eyeing Samantha closely.

"It's about the babies," Samantha answered, looking at each of them in turn.

"Babies?" Cindy repeated. "Not baby?"

Samantha nodded. "Tor and I are going to have twins," she informed her friends. "There are going to be two little Nelsons running around Whisperwood. So we're short one crib!"

"Oh, my gosh," Ashleigh said, sitting back in her chair, her eyes wide.

Christina leaped to her feet and dashed around the table to fling her arms around Samantha. "Twins!" she exclaimed. "You're going to have twins!"

"Double the fun," Cindy said, smiling across the table at Samantha and Tor.

After their celebration dinner, Ashleigh, Christina, and Cindy left, chatting excitedly about the prospect of twins as they climbed in the car.

Samantha and Tor went back to the nursery again, and Samantha gazed at the room. "All the furniture fits perfectly," she said. "There's just the right amount of room for the other crib right there." She pointed at a space near the window. "It's going to be the perfect bedroom for our two little Nelsons."

"Stay right there," Tor said. "I'll be back in a second."

When he returned, he was carrying two champagne glasses filled with bubbly liquid.

"What's this?" Samantha asked, eyeing the glasses. "I can't drink any champagne, you know."

"It's sparkling apple cider," Tor explained. "We need to have a toast."

"A toast," Samantha repeated. "To our wonderful, loving family and friends, the future of Whisperwood, and the two newest members of the Nelson clan."

"And to us," Tor said, slipping his arm around Samantha's waist and raising his glass. "The two luckiest people I know."

Liverpool, March 30, 1974. Red Rum, with Brian Fletcher in the saddle, being led in by his trainer Donald "Ginger" McCain at Aintree after becoming the first horse since Reynoldstown in 1935–36 to win the Grand National in successive years.

RED RUM

1965–1995

Steeplechase's greatest champion, Red Rum, was born in 1965 in County Kilkenny, Ireland. Rummie, as he was called, ran one hundred races over a ten-year period. He won three flat races, three hurdle races, twenty-one steeplechases, and placed second thirty-seven times. The big bay horse's trainer, Ginger McCain, galloped him in the surf of the sea to help overcome a foot condition and to toughen his tendons.

Red Rum won the Grand National Steeplechase two years in a row, placed second the next two years, then won his third Grand National by twenty-five lengths. A foot injury ended his career, and after his retirement, Rummie made many celebrity appearances. When he died in 1995, the Grand National's only three-time winner was buried in a special grave next to the winning post at the Aintree racetrack, home of the Grand National.

Mary Newhall spent her childhood exploring back roads and trails on horseback with her best friend. She now lives with her family and horses on Washington State's Olympic Peninsula. Mary has written novels and short stories for both adults and young adults.